The Blacks of Cape Town

The Blacks of Cape Town

A NOVEL
by C.A. Davids

First published by Modjaji Books (Pty) Ltd in 2013
PO Box 385, Athlone, 7760, Cape Town, South Africa
www.modjajibooks.co.za

Cover artwork by Jesse Breytenbach
Book and Cover Design by Monique Cleghorn
Editor: Karen Jennings

Set in 11 pt on 15 pt FF Scala

Printed and bound by Megadigital

ISBN: 978-1-920590-38-3

ARTS &
CULTURE
TRUST

For my mother
Marjorie Combrinck (Davids)

Zara Black's Family Tree

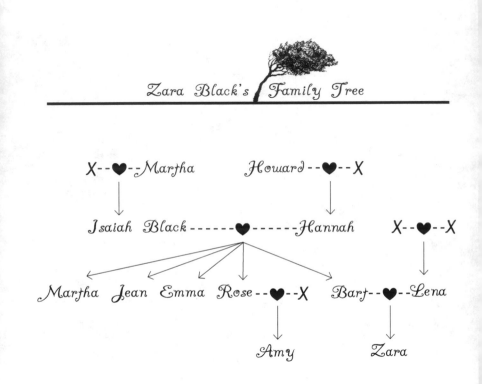

I

The music drifted in.

Up the lacquer-stained steps it went, two at a time, crept beneath the bedroom door and found Zara where she lay in the centre of the darkened room.

"*Round Midnight* ..." She heard herself before she realised she was speaking. Zara opened her eyes warily and sat upright. No, it could have been no other, only that song called her back to the places she loved.

Thirty two days and thirty three nights had passed. Zara counted each one despite the fact that she had tried to shut out memories of home. Had tried and failed. But then, she had fled a continent, a country and a place filled with life. My life, Zara thought, wiping away the last bits of sleep. She angled her legs from the single metal bed and stepped onto the cool floor. Letting loose her hair, Zara unlatched the window to let in the music and the chill air flowing up Bloomfield Avenue.

For the first time in a month Zara let her mind navigate easily, back to the city across the ocean, to the house where her heart was still marooned. It stood as solidly as it had for a hundred years. Squares of white stone, yellowing in the Cape Town sun, green tin roof rattling only occasionally, as it caught a channel of cool mountain air. *That* wind had been death to her roses, she remembered hearing her Ma Hannah say as she tended her garden, all dedication.

But after years of neglect, the garden had shrunk to nothing, so that stringy brown branches limped towards the gate. Trees that had stood eight foot tall, blooming in multitude, stooped low over the earth.

"*Round Midnight* ... Thelonious Monk's gift to the world," her father Bartholomew had said to himself as he dared the clouds to rain, that day years earlier. Back and forth, back and forth, he'd rocked on the family home's *stoep*, chewing heartily on the song, while his false teeth flapped to a rhythm all their own. Bart stopped the frenetic motion of the chair only long enough to tell Zara wild stories of stolen diamond fortunes and betrayal so macabre, he had said, it would melt her heart.

"Blarry hell, Sha Sha, you will never believe. Twice we betrayed: one necessary evil, the other wrong, plain wrong. Like father like son. Apple doesn't fall far from the tree. Rotten tree that it is. Sha Sha, you will never believe."

He had grown old too quickly, Zara had thought, as she stroked Bart's head.

In another city, on Bloomfield Avenue, in a town somewhere in Northern New Jersey, as other men hummed along to the music of their youth, Zara realised that if she had listened more carefully, she might have heard. Perhaps, then, she might not have been a fugitive from her own existence.

The white envelope embossed with the South African government seal had arrived one day. The letter had named her father – the *late* it had said, as if in the afterlife he was still arriving fifteen minutes behind schedule – among the traitors, conspirators and betrayers of their time. Not in so many words, but the letter had said so nonetheless. And not even a disbelieving child could un-write the words or undo the instinctive knowing that it was true. Hadn't Bart said so himself – two betrayals, not one? Zara did not have the stomach for it. Nonetheless, an account of Bart's life was catching up with her and would be retold in newspapers, on street corners, between considered pauses on television news. Would the whole story be told leaving out nothing, she wondered? But how could it?

After all, it had begun with her grandfather, Isaiah Black. Perhaps she would commence writing her account there, stretching back into history, going beyond and before herself.

Zara turned from the open window, walked to the mottled wooden desk and flipped open her computer. Gathering up memories like fragments of light, Zara began to write the story as only she could. A history – she knew this – in all its convoluted madness, shifting recklessly. But, what else could she do? It fell to her.

*

Family lore had it that Zara's grandfather, Isaiah, had thrown a shadow on three generations' worth of Blacks. Yes, the surname. *The surname.* That had its story, and it was not without irony. After all, Isaiah had chosen this name. But there were reasons, which had to be explained.

Isaiah was born on the cusp of a pernicious madness. The sort that started in men's chests and left them gasping for air, filled their heads so that there was no space for sense, and quickly spread to their feet, sending them rushing off in all the wrong directions. That madness was diamond fever.

It was also said that Isaiah was born in a town not yet known as Kimberley. And that Scots, Englishmen and Americans flocked by the boatload, Boers rushed on horseback and Africans ran there on foot. So it had been since 1869 when The Star of Africa, 83.5 carats of diamond, had been found on a farm close to the Vaal River. Men, women and children congregated in this place that was really no more than a hole in the ground, but which, as luck would have it, would one day become known for a massive hole in the ground.

*

There stands Martha: Isaiah's mother and Zara's great grandmother (who must always be remembered with a sense of solemnity) cooking before an open flame and eyeing the blackening clouds gathering overhead like trouble. Martha had found what she could at the market that day – whatever was available fresh, or at least, not yet decayed: meat from a skinny goat, green potatoes and near black tomatoes. It would have to do for a stew, she decided. But then, what did Zara know of this strange, sad woman in home-sewn skirts for whom there was no evidence? No gravestone, no pictures, or letters, or bits of clothing or any sort of trinket to prove that she had stood in the centre of these recollections? All Zara had were memories of memories.

Still, Zara worked with what she had.

There was Martha cooking. The mine workers arrived, queued around the shack and carried away plates piled with hot food. They always ate every mouthful.

After the men had been fed and young Isaiah wiped the stack of dented plates with a damp cloth (water was scarce and hygiene even more so), they sat outside, Martha holding a half-mug of liquor, brewed from the skins of potatoes in one hand and a needle in the other. She also sewed and darned socks at a small price for men who worked on the mine, some whose feet were so filthy and rotten that she had to soak the dismembered socks in vinegar before she would even touch them. At least, that was how it had to be remembered: Zara's great grandmother, holding the socks at arm's length, raising her young child alone and the only way she could – with a modicum of duty-bound disgust.

"'n Man se voete vertel jou alles – everything men's feet speak," she said roughly translating into English, a language that she insisted Isaiah speak. And Martha would have known what she was talking about as she sat on the edge of a rock, her cotton skirts shoved between her legs.

"What kind of man never wash his socks, but know how to get it fix when one potato break loose? I'll tell you what kind of man, my boy," she said as Isaiah drew circles in the brown sand and listened. "A man who don't care about others. Don't care who have to pay for his comfort. Don't care who have to clean his mess. Diamonds, and other hidden goeters – men, they can do anything if the beast is loose. See ..." She shoved Isaiah gently with her elbow, her finger pointed toward the mine. "Look what men do to others." Then came the prediction that he had heard many times before, but never like this: "Every day you see it more. One or two take everything because they think it belong to them. Think they're God's favourites. Idiote! Ask any woman – any woman will say all men are the same. Look ... they walk like lords, while other men are kept in that hole." Rising, pinched socks in one hand and mug in the other, Zara's great grandmother muttered, "The worst will come."

*

This was the Kimberley into which Isaiah was born. It was a place to which Cecil John Rhodes would one day arrive and where the imperialist, that worldly dreamer of a railroad from Cape to Cairo, would scheme and deal until he had control of one of the richest diamond mines in the world.

As for Isaiah's mother Martha, well, inevitably she would be a casualty of that hard mining town.

Yes, that was how Martha would be remembered – virtuous and knowing – to counter the fact that her child, her very own child, would in time, turn against her too.

2

The radio came to life in a series of sharp electronic stutters at 7am, as it had every day for the past two months. Zara reached limply from beneath the blankets, felt her way across the small table that held nothing but a radio and an unopened bible that had been there when she arrived, along with the colourless blinds and aerial picture of Northern New Jersey. Her hand found the button and shut down the talk of war and the coming elections. No, not today, she decided.

Unfolding herself, Zara climbed out of bed and made her way slowly across the room. There was no urgency in her world any more. No students with hollow sleep-deprived eyes waiting at her office door demanding to know why she had given them an upper second rather than a first grade pass. No administrative duties building up on her desk so that the pile was seconds away from becoming a paper avalanche across her office floor. She would prepare no lectures today, nor rush through a late afternoon session with her colleagues so that she could leave half an hour earlier to meet her cousin for coffee. Only an empty office waited somewhere in the cold distance.

Zara navigated blindly across the room, stopping only when she caught sight of her reflection in the bathroom mirror. She stared flatly at this stranger, and wondered why the face in the mirror could not smile. How pale she was, Zara noticed running a hand across her skin. The dark circles, yes, those she recognised. The impressions beneath her eyes were those of her four aunts on her father's side, Zara thought, pushing against the soft flesh with her finger. And of her mother? Of her beautiful, long-departed mother nothing remained, only memories, and those so rehearsed she could no longer tell fiction from truth. Zara's mother: the lovely Lena, teacher of biology and science, with her delicate hands and steely determination, had died of cancer when Zara was twenty years old.

Had her mother's hair been black or dark brown? Some days she could almost hear her mother's voice, the precise tone, and yet, such a clear detail as hair colour she had simply, stupidly forgotten.

Zara continued to dream of far-off places as she washed in the dark, and when she stumbled to the narrow counter that split the room in two, she found nothing in the food cupboard but a lone yellow apple to accompany her black instant coffee. Afterwards, she wrapped herself in her only woollen coat, stepped into the autumnal breeze and started down Bloomfield Avenue, in a suburb of Northern New Jersey.

The building that she walked from, 780 on Bloomfield, was a handsome turn of the century building in the Spanish Mission style, or so the advert on the internet had said. The walls were a pimpled white beneath overhanging red roof tiles. Black curled iron bars kept out peeping toms, an array of intruders and all sorts of unsavoury types that the news was always warning about. *The News at Ten* the night before had had such a feature: "Ten observations that could save you from your neighbours." Apparently one in ten was likely to be a sex offender while five in ten were bound to be shoplifters, sex addicts, drug addicts, food addicts or would-be Islamic terrorists.

Zara didn't think her neighbours were any of those.

It was just after Zara reached home from work, when the light had not yet retreated entirely, that she needed to hear children playing or feet shuffling down the brown-stained corridors. Instead the evenings were frighteningly peaceful. Yet when she placed her head on the pillow each night and tried to close out thoughts of home and the story that she had to tell, only then did the building awake and the shut, numbered doors began to reveal the depths of activities behind them. Someone flipped channels till the early hours of the morning, someone's child had nightmares, someone else awoke at 1:30 every night to use the bathroom and didn't flush or wash their hands. The couple next door hadn't had sex for two weeks. Zara knew because when they did, the paper thin walls revealed the plumbing of their married lives. Zara never looked at the couple when they got into the lift with her.

That morning, Zara met none of these people in the deserted, dark corridor.

She walked past the store adjoining her building and as always heard the greeting before she saw the store owner.

"My friend, my friend. What lovely weather this is, wouldn't you say?" He always came hurrying to the front of the store to catch Zara as she went by, his limp most noticeable when he rushed. The man's silver hair was combed heavily to one side and his still thick moustache – a spirited black – was fluffed and buoyant like a feather duster. He always spoke about the weather and didn't seem to mind that Zara always responded with the same curt reply.

"Yes, lovely. Good morning, Mr Ortez." At least she assumed that was his name. That was what the sign on the storefront read: *Ortez and Sons, Quality Tobacco Merchants since 1950.* Was this Ortez the original? Zara wondered as she walked on, and was Junior waiting patiently or even impatiently somewhere in the wings? Or could this be the son whose life had so carefully, so distantly been laid out for him? She walked past the cluster of restaurants: Indian, Moroccan, Ethiopian, Thai and Vietnamese, already sending their spicy, sweet odours into the morning air to lure an early crowd.

"We make the third world more palatable," the owner of the Ethiopian restaurant had said mockingly one evening as Zara found herself searching for a place to eat.

"Come, sit, we bring the rest of the world to you in nice bite-sizes, so you don't have to get your shoes dusty ..." he'd said, teasing and taunting the crowd of students and lecturers as they apologetically acknowledged the little they knew about his homeland and agreed they were not likely to visit anytime soon.

When the owner of the restaurant happened upon Zara, a fellow African, he had embraced her like an old friend, before quietly admitting that he too had never visited Ethiopia, having been born and raised in New Jersey. She passed the restaurant now, stopping at the coffee shop at the corner, where she ordered her second dose of caffeine for the day. Steaming paper cup in hand, she walked beneath overhanging trees, past the junior school that revealed the changing face of the area even more than the global eateries; past the same ancient man that she saw every day, who much like the oak in his garden, appeared to be rooted to the spot, until she reached the park and her usual place on the bench overlooking the green: a neat bit of land that stood before a forest of magnificent trees.

At the start of autumn the leaves had turned the softest auburn. But each day thereafter the trees became more agitated, growing bolder and louder until all that remained were forests caught up in mass hysteria – oranges, reds, purples. Complete madness.

The Cape's autumn by contrast had always been mild and uneventful. At the worst, cardigan season; no more than an inconvenient passing from summer to winter. Unlike the North there was no turning of leaves to unimaginable colours. Zara pulled her coat tightly around her, felt the wind lift her hair off her shoulders and wondered what would happen next. It had been two months since she had received the letter from the government announcing that documents once sealed would soon be declassified and that her father's name was amongst those whose deeds would finally be known, for history to judge. What those acts were had not been said. So it had been two months in which she had packed up all her things, moved across the world, and yet nowhere had she seen her father's name – not in newspapers that she scoured online. Not on television or radio programmes that she listened to each day. Ritualistically, she did an internet search on her father's name each morning, terrified of the day that she would find it and yet somehow hoping that when the truth was uncovered, at least it would be over. She didn't know what to expect, the letter had given her no clues as to what this betrayal might be. All she knew, could determine from it, was that her father had done something in his past to earn him a dubious reputation amongst the current government. Something which made him, at the least, appear to be a traitor.

It was precisely this matter that had taken her to Pretoria to meet with a government official at his offices, days after she had received the letter. She had waited uneasily in the carpeted lounge;

rooms like those – official, officious, a distinct whiff of authority or perhaps leather seats and floor polish, and a picture of the country's president watching her every move – made her hands go clammy and cold. When she finally made her way into the office, Zara had walked towards a man seated behind his desk, his gold tie perfectly knotted, his beige suit impeccable and his hair shimmering and immaculately coiffed. He had beckoned her to sit.

"Miss Black," he had said, and looked at her with an open sort of mocking. "I am very busy, but I thought I would meet with you because you were asking my secretary too many questions," he'd smiled, paused, and straightened his tie. "I think it is quite clear, your father was involved in something untoward," he had continued flatly. "No, we do not have the wrong man. No, we did not make a mistake. I'm sure that's what you've hoped for and perhaps I can understand that. But it is you who will be disappointed if you pursue this matter. As for the proof you keep asking for ... well, unfortunately for now that is all still classified and I couldn't possibly allow you access to those documents. You will know the details when the rest of the country knows. We notified you out of courtesy, so you could prepare for the time when the information is finally released. No, my dear, you must accept the hard, cold truth. Your father had secrets," he'd said. "Thank you for coming," the man had risen, showing her from his office.

Aside from the official letter from the government to Zara, there had been a rectangle of news in a daily paper reporting that names of traitors and betrayers would someday be released.

It was then that Zara had begun to scrutinise the papers, day-in and day-out waiting for the time when she would know what the claims against her father were. But aside from this, there was neither further news, nor an explanation forthcoming. Why the names would be released at all was not known to her.

*

Zara checked her watch. It was time to get going. She had accepted the postdoctoral position at the University of Berwick soon after she had received the news about her father. She barely remembered applying. Occasionally, fate did still work in mysterious ways, she thought, preparing to walk the hill to her office.

3

It was scant comfort, this writing of a history. And it took its toll, because the excavating of a story that Zara knew only through others did not come easily. But then, also a scholar of history, Zara boldly located her family within its annals. This was how Zara occupied her days. To stop the thinking, and longing. So after the hours crooked over her desk going through translated documents from Timbuktu, or articles from other researchers, she walked home, and then over a sandwich or a can of heated soup (which Zara had begun to think of as one of the world's great contributions to scholarship) she began where she last left off. Or, she backtracked and changed everything, the recollection altering again as she did so. She had a life to construct. Her own possibly. But that would still come.

What she knew about her Grandfather Isaiah was this: he had fucked up generations to come.

*

Kimberley: and under the slight but charismatic Englishman, mines were slowly bought up and soon the place would become the location for the most powerful diamond cartel in the world. Like the Kimberley dust that got in everywhere, surely stories must have settled in Isaiah's ears about vanishing prospectors, diseases intentionally ignored and private wars waged between the godfathers of the mine? New laws had taken hold of Kimberley, under British authority. Itsy-bitsy pieces of flyaway paper could command that a man stop in his tracks, and these passes drew invisible lines in the powdery sand, preventing grown men from travelling to certain places, while curfews were implemented and all sorts of restrictions became the norm. At least for some. Anyone who was not visibly European or Afrikaner – that is to say, starting with anyone whose skin revealed a dark blush beneath, or whose bridge amply crossed a face, or whose lips rose to a full moon when closed – was no longer permitted to move freely or allowed too close to the diamonds. Those who could – and there were many – crept beneath the fence to the other side.

There were many stories in that place called Kimberley. Some Zara knew without having to verify, though she did nonetheless. One Saturday morning in the University of Berwick's expansive African library, she came across an ancient book filled with yarns and facts. In the *Kimberley of Cecil John Rhodes* by W.W. Strobe, she read the author's impressions on first entering the town.

It had taken W.W. Strobe weeks of travel from England and then bruising days spent on horseback until finally he reached somewhere. The place, to Strobe, seemed to materialise from nothing but presented thousands of men, women and children covered from head to toe in a shroud of fine golden dust living in a labyrinth of tents and iron shanties. Moving deeper in, he found ramshackle pubs named for fallen heroes (he had quenched his thirst at Nelson's Eye, the King James Tavern and Napoleon's Sorrow), produce markets where anything could be bought or bartered and where every instance of human being sorted, sifted and carried beneath a sun that was said to have been its own curse. Whole families, Strobe reported, counting ten or more, sieved sand through metal dishes, and young boys genuflected beneath the gaze of their pipe-smoking, turbaned elders. The diggers seemed immune to the stench of rot that drifted off dead horses and cows that had been left where they had died along the roads. But W.W. Strobe felt the sickening odour move through his body and reach into his stomach.

At the epicentre of all this frenetic motion, Mr Strobe found a plethora of voices and languages: Scots, Zulu, English, Xhosa, Afrikaner and Griqua (at the back of the book he had made extensive notes about the etymologies of the languages he did not know). Men were shouting commands to other men who, in a haze of dust and heat, vanished into the largest hand-dug excavation on earth, already then at 215 metres deep and 17 acres wide. Bodies everywhere climbed on and off ladders, hauling buckets filled with dirt.

Strobe heard from the locals that the summer months were the worst, when rain and wind came down with such force that tents took off in the middle of the night. The wind grabbed hold of men at the scruff of their necks and shook them about while lightning and rain beat down for hours and days. Once the rain finally dried up, disease came: typhoid, dysentery and scurvy took as many lives above ground as did the collapsing earth beneath.

Zara scanned the pages of this strange little hardback (parts diary, travel journal and historical record) until she came across a rhyme or anecdote that she imagined Isaiah must have known, because he was there when it was first conceived.

Jan, Jan where did the diamond go?
Up your nose, or in your shoe,
Or tucked away in mama's stew?

That was how it went, because one, Jannie Daniels, had done the unthinkable. According to legend, Jannie, a well known character in Kimberley, was a man built for war with shoulders so broad that he always turned sideways on entering a house, meaty hands that sat at the end of his arms like sledgehammers and height so extraordinary that he never once met a man face to face. Jannie swallowed a diamond the size of the black mole on his neck and got away with it as well. Only, the diamond was never found. Jannie waited days, weeks and quite frankly never knew when it was time to give up. Waiting patiently, eating a diet meticulously composed of rough bread and vegetables (for ease of effort) he squatted over a metal plate and waited for a new life to sound beneath him. It never came. Could be that Jannie missed his chance, and yet, how could his roving fingers and thorough eyes overlook his one big break in life? According to Mr Strobe, years later, long after Jannie had lost control of the precious few faculties he had left, he could still be seen walking around the town telling people about his riches.

"... I shit diamonds, just take a look ..." he said, the only twinkle coming from his demented eye. Children laughed and delicate women closed their ears in disgust. But some smiled sympathetically and nodded.

Flipping through the same book, Zara learned of other accounts of diamond theft. Teeth were allowed to rot in order to provide a soft, safe haven for gems. Young women, employed to clean the diamonds, hid them in the recesses of their own bodies – men too. But the mine owners, themselves tempted enough by the stones to do anything, appointed men whose duty it was to find the stolen gems. They looked in shoes, under armpits, up nostrils, and yes up anuses too, because they knew everyone was desperate for a piece of this treasure.

Zara's grandfather, having heard of such acts and being one who never could bear the machinations of his body (despite the betrayals to come, Zara gave him this), realised that he would have to find another way if he were ever to break free of the mines. Once he had committed to this idea, the size of the act was not in question.

This was the Kimberley in which Isaiah had become a man. By the time he turned sixteen the twentieth century had almost dawned, and with the dreary years of education at the local missionary school complete, Isaiah went in search of work. He must have chosen his clothes carefully for his first day: a starched white shirt and a pair of good black pants bought from savings assiduously collected over the years. And laced tightly to his feet so that they would not fall off? Perhaps, Zara decided, a reminder of Isaiah's father: a shined-up pair of black shoes that his father, the philanderer, had been in too much of a rush to take with as he scuttled off into the distance, barefooted and shamefaced, on the night that Martha discovered his infidelity.

And Martha? Well, her story would end sadly, of this Zara was certain. Isaiah had to look beneath him to find his mother because each year Martha sank a little deeper into herself. She no longer cooked for grateful miners nor darned their socks. Instead she fed the precocious pie-holes and cleaned up after Kimberley's well-to-do children. Many more things had changed on the mines and her prediction had long rung true. The sole prospector, carrying his possessions around the world in search of a windfall, had disappeared. The city of tin and wood, too, was gone. In its place standing sentinel was a building of cement and brick, beside that a compound surrounded by fences, dogs and a watchtower. On the rim of the mining town stood the neglected, thrown-together homes where Isaiah and Martha lived.

Isaiah stared at his shoes. The Scot asking the questions had taken to wearing his orange hair unkempt, covering most of his face and visible skin. McDonald (Could that not have been his name? Zara wondered). Yes, McDonald, cleared his throat and in a soft and melodious voice asked Isaiah if he could read and write.

"I can do a bit of both, sir," Isaiah answered politely.

"Sounds 'bout right. What else can you do then? Strong are you?"

"Yes, sir. I can work long hours, lift and carry. I also know some arithmetic."

"Write your name down here," McDonald struck a sheet of paper with a blackened finger nail, while Isaiah took the pencil and did as he was told.

"You from around here?"

"No, sir. My father is dead, and my mother too, sir," Isaiah replied, looking down as he told his first lie. "I'm here to find honest work."

"Nothing like it, son. You start tomorrow, six in the morning. You will help in the offices, order supplies, keep an ear out for anything going on, make tea and so on. We'll see how you fare. That's where we work sorting the stones and getting them ready for the merchants. Now – you're not to let anyone through these doors. And you don' enter that room, ever," McDonald said, pointing to the metal door at the end of the corridor. "No late coming, and absolutely no talking with the natives."

"Yes sir," Isaiah answered, and left through the door reserved for gentlemen.

Zara had a clear picture of her grandfather as he emerged on the other side of that door: no longer the innocent, he was a man set on his path. Isaiah stepped into the sunshine and into the sunny half of Kimberly – where doctors, librarians, murderers, circus performers and their troupes wheeled and dealed, conned and connived. Where gabled houses stretched down roads, and where pubs spat out drunkards into streets illuminated by electric lighting that the British had built to light their way on the dark continent.

It was on the dark half that Isaiah turned his back; where misery and bitterness drew from each other, where men lived hundreds to a room and spent their days underground. With each step, Isaiah walked away from the township, and soon he too was fashioned like the men who wore Oxford tweeds, neatly pressed flannel trousers and London-bought bowler hats, fat and smooth.

In the one photograph that Zara had seen of her grandfather, he was seated upright in a wingback chair. A slim, fair man with a softness that made him seem considerably less wicked than his reputation had made him out to be. His clothing: neat, precise.

Surely with his appearance complete, Isaiah would have paid attention to his accent. In an attempt to shake off whatever had not already fallen off, he smoothed his A's and rounded his R's, levelling the field. Then he sought alternate accommodation.

*

And what did family lore say of Martha? Her historical record was unblemished.

Martha could carry a sheep on her back and slaughter the terrified thing without getting a drop of blood on her newly washed skirts, or squat for hours as she dug up onions from the earth. Her face, though still lovely in its way, must have been tired after a life of toil, and no doubt would have echoed the sun-etched lines of all those before her who had worked the land and had spent too many days outside.

Of course, Martha had met heartbreak. Zara imagined it had found her in the middle of the night, when her eyes were closed, her body weak with love for the father of her son. But it was not her name that he, Isaiah's father, called as his body went rigid and his concentration waned (Zara looked quickly at this whisper of a great grandfather, and then that was all, she had seen enough). Another woman might have waited for the moment to pass, or convinced herself that she had heard wrong, been mistaken. Martha was no such woman. No, she was righteous (Zara maintained) and so naturally she kicked the scoundrel out before she could change her mind and, watching him go, swore to remember the taste of deceit.

In her son becoming a man, who knew Martha would meet heartbreak again? She guessed why Isaiah only visited at the end of the month, when the day was gone, or why he spent only a solitary hour in her company. She found a million reasons for why her son would suggest that they ignore each other should they accidentally meet in town, but feared only one. A mother knows, and even back then at the start of a new century, in a town at the bottom of the world, there were to be no exceptions to this universal norm. Isaiah had made the decision years earlier (staring at his feet as McDonald scoured his face) – that he would walk in his father's shoes after all. On the outside Isaiah would wear the high bridged nose and pale English skin that his father had left him.

Unseen: a life-long regret that he had made his mother feel ashamed of her own dark skin.

4

The campus of the University of Berwick was vast and inhospitable. All concrete, brick and metal, it took the term 'urban campus' a little too seriously, Zara thought, as she made her way towards her office overlooking the sculpture that climbed ten feet into the air – limbs and spirit striving with academic purpose. She was meant to be sharing her office with someone, but had seen no sign of the other woman yet. In fact, she had barely spoken with anyone since first arriving. Still, to balance her nightly appointment with her own history, she had her work, her research. She unlocked the door and pushed it open with her free hand. It was Zara's study into hot and arid Timbuktu that kept her sanc. The fabled name of impossible places where, as a child, she believed everything and nothing existed. Only as an adult did she come to realise that the place indeed existed and not only that, it carried a legacy that was slowly revealing itself. As a historian she wanted to learn more.

The University of Berwick's scholarship, offering eighteen months of contemplation and silence to mull over some of Mali's already translated and digitised ancient scrolls, had come to her attention via a colleague. Timbuktu's scrolls were proving to be the most exciting historical find amongst local scholars – hundreds of thousands of works, some dating back to the thirteenth century, were waiting to be explored. Everyone in the history world wanted to be close to the action.

Timbuktu. In that hot, arid and still place on the fringes of the ever-encroaching Sahara Desert, buildings rise from the sand. The city had once been a place for scholars with libraries packed with books and scrolls, but it was also where Africa had traded with the rest of the world. It was the stuff of legends and impossible stories had surfaced like the one about Timbuktu's Mansa Mussa who in 1324 had carried 180 tons of gold with him across Africa on his pilgrimage to Mecca, devaluing the Egyptian currency in the process. Anyone who had ambitions of a career as a historian was interested in Timbuktu.

But then, while generous, the scholarship in New Jersey was hardly impressive. It would afford the recipient a furtive and distant glance at a hot find. Zara had applied nonchalantly, not actually wanting it, and gave the matter no further thought until she won her place just days after receiving the letter about her father. She had accepted the period of study gratefully; a few strings pulled and many pleading emails later, she secured her papers and permits from the U.S. consulate within weeks.

*

With Timbuktu still on her mind, Zara pulled on her coat, stepped into the corridor and made her way down the passageway that was lit with row after row of anodyne lighting, casting everything in a pallid mood.

The nearest cafeteria was wall to wall with students eating, working and chatting. Zara searched for an open table. To her left was a group of girls in headscarves working studiously between mouth-fuls, and to her right a mixed cluster of males and females, in loud conversation, their torsos bouncing as they passed around an iPod, the lyrics discernible despite the headphones: something about *staking, partaking, never faking.* Zara made her way to a table at the furthest reach of the cafeteria, empty, owing to a crooked leg that left it hanging precariously.

Raising a forkful of the rice salad she had selected from the campus cafeteria's offering of mostly pizzas, burgers or pastas, Zara wondered why she could not stop looking back. Of course, she knew the answer. Her mother had died when she was twenty and remembrance had taken special significance, being that it was all Zara had. Disparate and lawless, the memories showed up when they wanted, vanishing just as quickly if Zara did not stop whatever she was doing to pay attention.

Zara had made her father, Bart, repeat the story of how they had met, her mother nearly two decades his junior. Bart, a confirmed bachelor, half given-up and sad, could not believe that the young teacher might love him.

"Hell, Sha Sha, she could have chosen anyone, but she picked me. She was really something," her father had said that day, months before his death.

Her mother Lena had walked alone into a jazz club at the age of nineteen.

"What else?"

"She sat at the front table," her father continued.

"Not second from front?" Zara had teased, warming, as always, to the small details that never changed however many times this story was repeated. What certainty, what beauty in this certainty.

"She sat there, a fine-looking woman with a sense of herself. That was who she was. Ja, Sha Sha, that was who she was," Bart had said, perfectly still as he began to disappear right before her, so that it seemed to Zara that it was both parents she had lost rather than one.

Lena had bruised her knee on their first date. She had loved the colour orange. On their wedding day Lena wore a cream silk rose in her black hair, which was tied loosely into a bun at the side of her head. Zara replaced her fork and bit her lip. How could she have forgotten? Her mother's hair had been black, not brown like her own, she reproached herself, pushing away the rest of her half-eaten meal.

Lena, who had grown up beside the ocean, on a wide stretch of beach with white sands and cool waters; who had said that afterwards she was ruined for good. Her mother never could make sense of the asphalt suburbs and the absence of natural beauty after her family was moved to the city fringes. Lena had lived long enough to see Zara graduate with her first degree before submitting to the cancer that had started in her breast and worked insidiously through her body.

Without the recollections, Zara would have felt that much emptier.

As a child, Zara had been fascinated by the long complicated stories that her father had told about his own father. Her grandfather Isaiah had died before Zara was born; still, she knew details about his life from stories that passed to her, so that by the time she sat down to write them as a woman, far from home, the stories had taken on a sort of permanence – portraits of another era.

Of his own world her father had been less forthcoming – the trail of his life had vanished around the time he stopped practising law and only began after he had met her mother. She had always known that much was still missing and when she'd received the letter from the government declaring her father a traitor, Zara realised that it offered an explanation for those missing years.

With her lunch listlessly eaten, Zara headed towards the employment office of the university. The small airless room was at the end of another long, feebly lit corridor and housed several desks staggered around a square room, each occupied by someone earnestly at work.

For employment related matters Desk 3 read a handwritten sign at the entrance to the room. Zara checked that she had brought the relevant sheets of paper and that each, as per the instructions, had been dated and signed before she made her way to desk three. The Employment Officer looked up only long enough to take the batch of papers with one hand, and ushered Zara into a seat with the other.

"Let's see ... right ... right ... uh huh ... no ... no ... you didn't fill this out right," the woman said, shaking her head as the flesh beneath her chin wobbled accusingly.

"I didn't?" Zara asked, surprised. She was a stickler for certain things, especially the completion of forms.

"Where it says tick race-slash-ethnicity-slash-place-of-origin you left it blank," the woman answered, as her blonde head continued to sway disapprovingly.

"Yes, I know ..."

"Why?"

"Well ... urm ... I didn't really think it was necessary."

"It wouldn't be on the form if it wasn' nece-ssary," the woman answered vigorously as her colleagues' heads began to pop up from behind their computers, so that Zara got the distinct impression she was an innocent in perilous waters.

"Look, its personal, I just don't see the point ..."

"No honey, you look, if you don't tick it then I can't pay you and then in about two weeks' time you gonna be back standing right there, telling me I can't do my job. Just tick it so I can go to lunch," the woman said, yawning openly and checking her watch. Clearly her morning snack had worn off, thought Zara, surveying the black ringed mug and the empty saucer, not even a crumb visible.

Zara looked at the form again. She couldn't remember when last she had willingly filled out such a form.

- American Indian
- Alaska Native
- Other Pacific Islander
- Asian
- Black or African-American
- White
- Hispanic
- Native Hawaiian
- Some other race

"What?" Zara managed, not quite beneath her breath.

She read the form again, more thoroughly, reading the fine print where it was applicable.

Asian. A person having origins in any of the original peoples of the Far East, Southeast Asia, or the Indian subcontinent.

Her mother's family had been largely Asian; her maternal grand-father Indian.

Black or African-American. A person having origins in any of the original peoples of Africa.

One of her great grandparents, and probably countless others in her line had been African. But then, if one wanted to be argu-mentative, everyone had their origins in Africa.

White. A person having origins in any of the original peoples of Europe, the Middle East, or North Africa.

Another of her great grandparents had been British.

Zara tapped her pen against the page. It was precisely forms like these that she had rejected all her life. In fact, it had been her parents that had always encouraged her to snub such question-naires outright. Race had not been a matter up for discussion in their home. And this was what Zara wished to remember about her parents: their irrational, madly idealistic desire to raise a child unscathed by a country at war with itself.

"Don't refer to people like that Sha Sha," her father Bart had reprimanded her gently one day after school. "There are many ways to describe people and by the colour of their skin is just unimagina-tive ..."

"But Miss Osman said that we were coloureds and more respect-able ..."

"Oh, that woman is a bleeding idiot!" Lena had interjected. "*Mizz* Osman doesn't have a notion of anything beyond what she's been told."

"But you *did* say we were black and not coloured if asked at school," Zara had pushed ahead, intrigued by the inbuilt maze of her parents', and certainly her mother's, world.

"Yes. We did. And only because unity in this country is important. Unity and loyalty," Bart had added.

"Tell that paper-cut-out of a teacher not to indoctrinate children with her lunatic ideas," Lena had ended the conversation abruptly.

This simple act of refusing race a place in their home (as other families might ban swearing, or blasphemy) returned to her parents an otherwise denied humanity. Because race, as important as it was in South Africa, was also simply unimportant. And even when they were forced to declare race – black in unity, rather than *coloured* as they were technically classified – privately, Zara's parents still held the truth.

*

Zara looked at the form again. Some Other Race? What was that though?

"Look, I won't be filling this in," Zara decided, pushing the form back in the direction of the woman. The employment officer took a moment as if she were collecting herself. Zara felt the woman's eyes wander across her face, slowing as she reached Zara's full mouth, her eyes, hovering at the nose that Zara as a teenager had thought lacked delicate proportion, before the woman's eyes lingered on the hair that hung in waves to Zara's shoulders. The employment officer looked down, a chubby hand shielding whatever it was she was writing, before she stamped the forms hard with an officious red dye, and slid the forms neatly into the tray marked "Out" before saying dismissively beneath her breath, "Right, you're done."

Surprised, and altogether off guard, Zara stood, gathered her things and started for the door. Zara knew, before she even walked away, that what she should have done was catch the woman's eye, hold it for a second – the way Americans so pointedly do when they want to see the mark of the person they are dealing with – and protest. But instead Zara bit her tongue. It was an old habit she had learned somewhere along the line of losing an argument without saying a word.

5

When daylight passed, it was filled with this other world.

The reliability of Zara's research on Timbuktu and the idea of scholars around the world chipping away at a history that could be shaped and verified, offered its comforts, because Zara's own story presented its challenges. Some bits solid and reliable: names and dates and consequences with which Zara could construct a framework, while the canvas remained only half decided. Sitting down at her desk in her room on Bloomfield Avenue late in the evening, Zara checked the clock. Satisfied that her day was done, at least, that one part of her day had been crossed off, she looked onto the road beneath where she could watch the steady settling into night, cars becoming fewer, and a hush falling between the rows of strangers, their coats pulled tightly around hazy frames as they made their way home.

She had reached the point where it had to be told, as it had happened. The act that would not only determine her grandfather's fate, but which would, consequently, place him in proximity to her grandmother, so setting the scene for her father's entrance. Zara fiddled with her hair, tied it in a knot at the top of her head. Then she reached back to a summer's day in 1904 (Wasn't there perpetual sun in the olden days?). Isaiah's time had arrived.

*

McDonald, the supervisor at the mine office rushed towards Isaiah, his orange hair shivering like leaves in the breeze: "German merchants arriving in an hour and everyone's off sick or somewhere else. Check that all the diamonds are accounted for. They're our best stones. You'll help me out, won't you son? Every stone in the box should be in the book – check that they are all there. I should do it myself, but there's no time. Check carefully, it'll be my head if anything goes missing," he called out, frisking his pockets vigorously, as he raced towards the metal door beyond which Isaiah had not been permitted in four years. McDonald unlocked the door, opened the safe with a combination that only he and a few others knew, and brought out a box. Isaiah waited a moment to catch his breath, the weight of his fate balancing. When he heard the key turn in the lock and McDonald's shoes echo down the corridor and away, he knew precisely what to do next, because inside the first box was another, and within the confines of the second box were uncut diamonds. Isaiah tore out one of the three written pages within the book, and started to rewrite the entries onto a clean sheet, leaving out ten lines.

When McDonald's approaching footsteps came back into earshot, Isaiah had finished rewriting the entries, and had stowed the ten diamonds in his shoe. With the evidence of his crime still in his hands, Isaiah must have realised that there was only one thing to do. He stuffed the sheet of paper into his mouth, a wry smile starting at his lips and spreading through his body.

"Done, are you? Here they come," the Scot asked, popping his head around the open door.

Isaiah swallowed the mouthful of paper. "All in order, fifty-four carats as it says," he answered, rising from the desk and walking towards McDonald without a limp or hint of the deceit underfoot. He held the book open to the recently dried page and as McDonald stretched to take it, Isaiah dropped the book so that it hit the floor, closed. "Oh, what page, open the book to the page," McDonald said agitated as Isaiah fumbled to find the page. "Oh just leave it. I'm thankful to you. And thankful we rid ourselves of the shame of being searched – that they'd even try," McDonald said as they left the room together. "It's the native, after all, who has thievery on his mind. Straight off I'd refuse if anyone asked me to search a white man. And never a friend. That's why we told them, we did, 'You will not take a man's pride by checking his pockets like a common thief; not a white man', that's what we told them."

Were these McDonald's final words to Zara's grandfather as the Scot misunderstood the meaning of Isaiah's quiet smile and steady eyes?

"Thank you son, don' know what I'd do without you," McDonald said, a grateful smile hanging from his face as he shut the book and walked away.

6

What Isaiah did next was the act that left the stone in the Black family shoe. It had been the telling of *this* story that had always set Bart's jaw, and it was here that Zara's father first located the wicked family gene.

*

With a shoe full of diamonds, his bowler hat askew, his manner purposely nonchalant, Isaiah ambled slowly away from the mines until he was well out of view. Then he began to run. A man with much to fear, Isaiah knew what happened to diamond thieves. Those caught and tried were the lucky ones while a fate altogether more sinister awaited the rest.

Isaiah ran and only when he reached his mother's shack did he finally slow down. There he caught sight of Martha through the open door, seated at the kitchen table and staring at the ceiling as if in conversation with God.

"Boy, what you do?" Martha turned and asked, as she saw her son's face in daylight for the first time in four years.

"We must go! I can't explain now but we have to leave," he said, hobbling on one foot as he emptied the contents of his shoe onto the table.

As the stones tumbled from Isaiah's shoe like bits of dirt, Martha, virtuous and shamed, covered her eyes with frail brown hands.

"This is not what I want for you. Not this," she said quietly, the words leaving her lips as a futile prayer.

"Mama I did it for us, so we can leave here and have a better life," Isaiah said, softly.

"Son, my son," Martha said, still not looking up. "What curse you bring? And for what, stones? Little shiny things," she said, her anger growing. "For this things?" she said, in a fast moving fury, tasting a life of betrayals and perhaps the great treachery still to come.

"But what would you have me do?" Isaiah removed the other shoe and sat on the remaining chair at the table massaging his sore foot. "Mind my manners, hold my cap in hand and say 'sir' and 'master' in the place that I was born? Or ... or better still work for someone who doesn't even think I am human? I was born here, and you raised me to be more."

Martha pulled herself up to her full height. "My mother's mother was a slave," she began hesitantly. "My father *is gebore en het gesterf*, born and die, on the same farm – a slave with no chains. Can you believe? But me, I'm free, and you ... you were supposed to be freer than me," Martha said, before she turned away and began to tidy the spotless room.

"What would you have me do? Do you know what I've seen?" Isaiah stood as well now and began to follow his mother from corner to corner of the small room.

What might he have said in his defence, Zara wished to know?

"There is an invisible world in there where men, invisible men, risk their lives for these diamonds. Workers aren't allowed clothes in the mines, only flour sacks, did you know? And even these are taken away when they come up from the mines after a day or night of labour."

Was this his real reason, or was it the only thing he knew he could say aloud?

He continued: "Every single day the mine workers in their flour sacks file in behind each other as they walk the chamber back from the mines to their dormitories. Then, with guards watching their every move they're ordered to pile these little rags at the entrance to a huge room. And then the guards begin *their* work: 'Open wide boy,' they say, 'turn to the left, other way imbecile,' 'jump up', so any hidden diamond might pry itself loose, 'lift arms,' 'turn three-sixty degrees, in a circle, monkey,' 'splay legs, spread arse'. You don't know what I've seen, you don't know. Day-in, day-out for months they live this way, but not me."

Martha's response as she evaluated this son of hers? This being to whom she had given birth and then her entire life? Whom she knew to be dishonest, even dishonourable, yet whom she couldn't help but love.

"So, this make you a big man, a brave man? To hide behind your skin and be like them?" She pulled an old metal bucket from the cupboard and a slowly disappearing rag used to clean the floor. "Your father wasn't a good man, it's true. But he was bad like all men. *My* curse, not yours ... but he never took something that didn't belong him," she continued, her voice flexing as she spoke these last words. And then quieting herself she continued, "You must hide, and leave when it's safe."

"Come with. I won't leave you here."

"You left me long ago, my son," Martha said, smoothing her hands over his face before she went to collect water from outside.

By the time policemen arrived with dogs searching for diamond thieves, murderers and traitors, Isaiah had disappeared into the cracks of the township.

Two months later, after the police had stopped making their rounds, Isaiah and Martha walked under guard of darkness to the station. Only the harmonising of the mine workers as their songs of home rose from behind the walls of the compound could be heard. No one's interest was roused by the curious couple. Isaiah – long and thin, a peak cap on his head and a threadbare cardigan, had transformed into any local boy while Martha filled her space like a woman who would tolerate no trouble, and the two walked undisturbed.

"Mama, change your mind. There is still time," Isaiah said, in the silence that stood between them when the train arrived.

"I bring you so far, you finish the job on your own. Go my son, start again," Martha said, solemnly.

Before Isaiah stepped onto the train, he promised that when it was safe he would be back to fetch her. He watched as Martha walked away, tired and alone.

*

By the time Zara placed her final full stop, it was three a.m. She had written herself onto the page, at least her beginnings. That was the train that took Isaiah to Cape Town, into the arms of her grandmother, Hannah, and the union which gave rise to four girls and Zara's father, Bart.

Zara had written almost all that she wished to say about Isaiah. The ancient knowledge even now, a century later, held its sting. For here is the ultimate betrayal then: Isaiah never did return to Kimberley, and, he never saw his mother again.

7

Zara watched unrelenting layers of snow sculpt scraggly bushes, naked trees and beat-up old cars into works of art. She had awoken that morning and the snow was simply there, immaculate, knee-deep and earlier than expected. But this loveliness came at a price; the cold was so unbearable that she had abandoned her time in the park in the mornings and had sworn off walking to work most days, refusing to turn numb for the sake of fresh air and exercise. Instead, when she felt she could afford it, Zara took a cab to campus where she stayed indoors, leaving her office and research only when she needed a cup of coffee or soup to ward off the cold that entered persistently through the metal window frames.

Sitting at the desk in a room that was slowly becoming her office (she had arranged a pile of books on South Africa neatly in one corner, resurrected a dusty fern that had been left to the elements, and placed that in another corner), Zara drew her attention away from the wonderland just outside her window. She did a Google search on her father's name, and, coming up with nothing, rose so that she could make her way towards the second floor to deliver her first paper. She manoeuvred an armload of books, papers and her laptop carefully amidst the students moving in all directions through the corridor, found the elevator, an ancient thing that opened tentatively, and pressed the copper button for the second floor.

Her colleagues introduced themselves one by one, coming up to her as she fiddled with her laptop, preparing to project *South Africa and Racial Reconciliation at the End of the Twentieth Century* across the room.

"Ah, you're our second from South Africa," the first man in line said, as he smoothed a hand over a stomach that leaned so far over his belt it seemed likely to drag him down to the floor. "The first was ten years ago. Just after your new South Africa. Your country was on the right track then. Embracing the right way ... yes ... pity," he continued as he patted his gut. "What with all the big men of Africa nowadays, rogue democracy tendencies ... third world shenanigans ... we are watching you closely ..." he said, and winked a crusty eye at Zara before he moved off to help himself to a pastry and cup of coffee.

"Ignore him," another suggested, taking the previous man's place so quickly that Zara barely realised someone else was before her. "He's of the old guard. Still thinks Thatcher and Reagan were right about *Man Dela* being a terrorist ... thinks China and India are the rising threat on the other side of the world ... I mean when last did he check where his watch was made, or his computer – if he even uses one – or his polyester pants, right? Doesn't have a passport, they say ..." before this man too wandered over to the coffee machine.

"So glad you're here," the last in line greeted her hurriedly. "The real world," the woman with the bulging eyes and skinny long arms persisted just as the presentation was about to begin. Zara looked down, uncertain what this could mean. "We need more, much more input from developing countries," she said, and had

she just clucked, as she squeezed Zara's arm? "In fact, I was instru-
mental in getting scholarships launched on Vietnam, Cambodia,
Timbuktu ..." Then she too made the predictable journey towards
the beverages.

*

When Zara was done with her talk and a faint burst of applause
started at the front (the woman who had been last to introduce
herself had sat eagerly through the entire thing, unlike many of
her colleagues) and then spread slowly around the small room, Zara
surveyed her new colleagues. What a small fish, she understood.
What a tiny speck in this massive country with its oversized everything: food, cars, generosity, greed, genius, stupidity, war budgets.
It was a country about to embark upon a historic election. The radio
news that woke Zara each morning had not minced words. This was
BIG. It was the first time an African-American had come this close
in attempting a run at the presidency. It was historic, the news had
declared and not only that, it was GLOBAL. Because when things
happened in America they also happened everywhere else. When
Americans bought cars, everyone benefited. Jobs were created,
economies soared, and when America drove those same cars, even
the man who had screwed a bolt into the car's tyre in some remote
factory in Bangalore coughed, and when America sneezed, well,
everyone knew, the whole world got splattered. Conversely, when
things, however historical or awful happened in another part of
the world, like say the fall of apartheid or an earthquake that wiped
out half a population, well, let's face it, as a caller to one of those
radio talk shows where almost anything could be spoken had said:

If it doesn't affect me in my backyard, well then: It's. Just. Not. That. Important!

*

Zara packed her books, closed her laptop and made her way back to her office, relieved that this, the first ordeal, was over. How minutely infinitesimally irrelevant she felt. Nothing like the uninterested faces of one's new colleagues, and academics at that, to drive the point home. It was not that Zara was so naïve that she had expected any sort of welcome, or colleagues especially interested in her research, but the acknowledgement of her remote place in the universe, or her country's place on the map (and a country was not yet on the map until it had hosted some major world event, according to another news channel) was important, at least to her. All of this made Zara's ache for home real. How sorry she felt for herself as she walked back to her office. Because she even missed *her* university with *her* colleagues, misguided or not, who thought ... no, *knew*, their distinct purpose in the world despite what that same world thought of them. Zara went so far in her fit of wallowing to allow herself a memory of her neat duplex with its two small bedrooms and its view of that flat mountain. Of the prism of sunshine that pushed its way into her bedroom at ten on Sunday mornings. Her family's old house on a hill that she had made available to a local organisation as offices, but which she still drove home towards when she was distracted or purely nostalgic. She missed her books, music, possessions that she had thought mattered little till that very moment.

Zara reckoned she understood history in a way one could only understand a great love: with acceptance, patience and forgiveness. That is, until you realise your affections have been misplaced, and that was how Zara felt at that very moment. A little betrayed. By her family. By her country. By history itself. No, greatly betrayed. Was this where nearly a decade of hard work had landed her? On the dark side of the academic moon?

Then again, Zara decided as she returned to her desk, this was not a weep-worthy moment. Those she had experienced, and she knew that this was not one. Hadn't she lost a mother prematurely, and then a father?

What was that horrible lump in her throat that made her want to call her father a good-for-nothing-son-of-a ... It was because of Bart that she was here. God! Zara chastised herself before the idea was even fully formed. Her grandmother, above all, was blameless. It was all Bart. Then again, the truth of it was that she loved her father. This was not Bart's fault. But then of course it was and she knew it too. Or maybe it was the country itself that was at the root of the problem. A country that had once offered forgiveness, only for it to be withdrawn in time. Anyway what was his crime meant to have been? A betrayal? Of whom? The struggle? Why, when everything her father had seemed to believe was contrary to such an action? So wasn't Zara allowed a moment of loathing for this father and for that country that had made her pack her bags and travel away with shame at her back?

So it went for a good hour: the horror of Zara's anger rising like a many-headed monster. Until a quick and neat rap at the door ended her round with self-pity, and brought forth the dean and head of department.

"Zara, hi – good presentation – I caught the last part," Jan Thomas said, poking her head around the office door. Her voice was as neatly efficient as her yoga-toned body, though Zara was relieved that she remained only a talking head that morning.

"Yes, thank you," Zara said, calmly as ever, haphazardly picking up papers, to give the impression that she had absolutely not been twisting her head back and forth in her own hands. The dean regarded her with a moment of caution before she spoke again.

"How is your accommodation? The office? Facilities?" She left no space for any kind of response. "Your office will be shared soon … well as soon as we can settle a few matters …" Jan said, and looked around the room pointedly. "I'm off to an urgent meeting, but just wanted to say congratulations and welcome …" She disappeared as quickly as she had arrived, leaving Zara looking at the door, alone again and with more questions than she knew how to answer.

8

There was a memory, or perhaps a story based on a memory, that came to Zara clean and clear. She knew it down to its lace petticoats and satin ribbons. Her grandmother, Hannah, had first told it to her. Her father Bart, audience to the same set of recollections, had filled in bits and pieces along the way, of that first meeting when Isaiah, criminal grandfather, clapped his wicked eyes on the lovely Hannah. Had it been love at first sight, or not?

The way Hannah told it, Isaiah had watched her climb down from a horse and cart: an ankle, thigh, arm, until she'd descended completely, her face beneath a hat, a soft blouse that climbed up her neck and a skirt that brushed the pavement as she walked.

But no, Zara reasoned that this could not be true. Her grandmother had probably walked to the store, which was not very far after all. Either way, Hannah had arrived in the centre of Cape Town one morning to shop for a new pair of shoes or to collect something or other. Zara could no longer recall being told. But, *that* meeting was the starting point of a union that would produce the entire Black family.

*

Hannah steered her way through the Saturday morning rabble of Adderley Street until she opened the door to Isaiah's jewellery store. A small bell shivered as the heavy wood slid slowly closed behind her. Isaiah – his eye easily moved by the sight of a woman – watched as the girl made her way around the store. Hannah peered into the glass cabinets, occasionally bending closer to look at rows of pearl necklaces and gold drop earrings that lay behind the glass, before moving off, a little sigh indicating her boredom. Finally she stopped, and pointed an inquisitive finger at a heart-shaped golden locket.

"Oh this – well this is very special, as a matter of fact. Made in India and ..."

"Sir, I'm not so interested in its origins as its final destination," the girl said, her English rippling with the Afrikaans inflections that permeated her sentences and seasoned all her words. She raised her chin and eyes like black holes peered from a dusky brown face.

"Ahem," she cleared her throat, embarrassed at the stranger's stare.

"Please, won't you try it on?" Isaiah asked and dug into the cabinet to retrieve the locket.

*

Isaiah had found the store off Cape Town's busy main road shortly after arriving from Kimberley. To acquire the store, Isaiah must have sold most of the ten stolen diamonds. Not all, because still there were a few of those Kimberley diamonds in the family. Each of Isaiah's daughters (there were four) had received a diamond of two carats or more, set immodestly into a bed of red gold (for his daughter Rose) or with emeralds (for Emma), with sapphires for

Jean and quietly unadorned (for the equally simple Martha). As Zara could recall, to have seen any of her father's sisters without their stones was to see them unready for company. And for his son? Isaiah's bequest to Bart was the house that fell down the line, until even Zara owned a piece of her grandfather's crime.

Nonetheless, Zara knew that Isaiah must have arrived in the new city friendless, exhausted and dirty from the days of travel via train from Kimberley to Cape Town. He would have walked the streets of that town until he found a hotel obscured between better, cleaner buildings. After a bath, and a deathly sleep on a mattress that had been softened with the bodies and sins of countless people, Isaiah awoke to a new life and a new name. Diamond thievery was too regular an occurrence for any one thief to be pursued. Still, Isaiah changed his name.

Black, he decided, erasing a surname which to that day no one in the family knew. No one. Tossed aside, leaving no trace of Isaiah's mother.

Black? Zara wanted to laugh, but couldn't summon a sense of humour. Was it Isaiah's show of victory at a system that sought to reduce him? Or perhaps just his idea of a roaring joke to be carried down the line for eternity? Mixed. White. Black? Maybe.

Perhaps, as any newcomer might, Isaiah looked out the window and saw a place where worlds had collided, where earth, oceans and mountains met millennia earlier, in preparation for the merging of worlds to come. After all, it was to Cape Town that people were flung from the furthest points of the world map, to rub shoulders with dissenting locals: ladies beneath pale yellow parasols (from the North), dark women with flowing hair and bound ankles (from the East), holy men fleeing persecution (from France) and enslaved neighbours (from Mozambique and elsewhere on the African continent), their existence merging in blood and violence and love and fucking. The Cape of Good Hope.

When Isaiah stuck his head out of the window to get a closer look, surely he saw Table Mountain for the first time, its indigo-grey dominating the city. And what of the blue Atlantic that was certain to have been placid that morning, as though not a breath were being taken or exhaled anywhere in the city? Did he see what Zara missed more than she wished to acknowledge as she turned up the thermostat half a degree, and boiled water for another cup of coffee so that she could stick to the task at hand: houses that tumble down the mountainside, trees that etch a permanently windswept contour against the sky, blowing in the same direction as the South Easter, even on airless days, as that was sure to have been.

*

"I've seen you here before, Miss ... ?" Isaiah enquired.

"September," she replied shyly, turning away from him.

"Do you live somewhere close by?"

"Not too far ..." she said, and tricked a curl loose from beneath her hat as she feigned interest in something else.

"I rarely see such loveliness on Adderley Street," Isaiah ventured.

"Well today you have," she smiled and walked quickly out of the store.

"Wait – I thought you liked the locket." But she had already disappeared into the crowd moving down Adderley Street and left Isaiah with the locket in his hand and his heart in his throat.

Zara knew that it was months later that the two saw each other again, and quite by accident. Isaiah was a man in his twenties by then. What would he have been up to in all that time? Zara could only guess that Isaiah was likely to find himself in the District early one Sunday in a house he didn't recognise, beside a girl he couldn't remember meeting, after a Saturday night of heavy drinking.

"Hey wake up – time for you to pay and go," a girl with the hollow proportions of the malnourished said, as she kicked Isaiah awake.

"What? Pay what? Where am I?" Isaiah sat upright.

"Oh, sorry, sir. My manners ... can I bring you some coffee? Pay for fucking! Where you think you are? In a hotel?" The girl threw his pants at him and then his wallet.

"Thank you," Isaiah said embarrassed, as he swung his pants from one leg to the other and tried to dress quickly.

As Isaiah walked back to his single room on the other side of town, his head throbbing viciously, he stopped to watch a group of parishioners radiant in their Sunday pastels, sins freshly washed away. Of course, this sight would have reminded him of his virtuous mother, whom he had been planning to fetch from Kimberley. But he forgot quickly about Martha when he spotted the minister with his family.

This was how it really was, all fiction aside: when Isaiah saw Hannah for the second time, she was framed in the shadow of a church. This story, Zara knew to the smallest detail. It was a warm day, and there he stood, on the other side of the road, kicking the dust with his boot.

Hannah was one of three girls. Each more delicate than the next, pert little noses pointed away from the ground, long plaits tied with bows and a sense of the arcane that came from walking in the path of a holy man. None of them stopped to speak to their fellow parishioners, but parted the crowd until they reached their horse-drawn cart. As the vehicle started to move, Isaiah, who was cemented where he stood, smiled as Hannah's eyes found and acknowledged him.

Isaiah returned to the church the next Sunday. He had shaved and dressed in his good suit – a thin pin-striped grey, a blue tie and a hat that he removed as he walked into the wood-panelled sanctuary.

Isaiah knew even less about prayer than he did about courting a well-bred girl, but he did his best and rose when everyone else in the congregation did, sang when they did, mouthed words meaningless to him as the flock loyally answered the minister's calls and passed the plate as it circulated. Hannah, who knew a thing or two about the world already, pretended not to notice him that first day. So he returned the following Sunday to be rewarded with a glance. By his fourth visit to the church in as many weeks Isaiah was growing bored. Hannah had not even looked in his direction the previous week.

As the family walked past, he stepped into the aisle. "Father, my compliments on a beautiful service. Very thoughtful," he might have said, obstructing their path.

"Thank you. Always good to know someone is listening to my voice and God's thoughts. Have I seen you here before?" the minister answered, and surveyed the stranger carefully.

"Only recently. I moved to the Cape not too long ago, and what a blessing to find your church. Truly, I was blessed. Isaiah Black, from Kimberley."

"Uhh, girls," the old man undoubtedly stammered as he tried to draw his family around to meet a gentleman, clearly, of some taste. "I am Father September, this is my wife, these my daughters Florence and Christina, and this one is my niece, Hannah."

"Pleased to make your acquaintance, Madam." Isaiah took Mrs September's gloved hand and bowed genially. "Ladies," he bowed again and did he not then smile a moment too long in Hannah's direction?

"Black? I don't know any Blacks in Cape Town." A face that was said to be as cool and partial as the Cape's winter greeted Isaiah as Mrs September surveyed him from the end of her nose. According to Hannah her aunt did not have youth to beautify her, unlike her daughters, and unlike her daughters she thought she had no equal in the room, besides the doctor, the four teachers and possibly their families.

"No. I have no family here," Isaiah said, and feigned a pathetic look.

"Well then tea it is, Mr Black," Mrs September said, like a woman who had three girls to rid herself of and no time for games. "Three o'clock sharp Mr Black. Father will give you our address. Good afternoon. Girls!" And off they went, Hannah trailing behind, smiling shyly.

At one minute to three that afternoon Hannah heard a knock at the door. The house was a cold and quiet place with corners that absorbed light, pennies, and long forgotten needles that might have once fallen to the floor.

Isaiah was welcomed into the main room by the minister as a heavy brass hand of a standing clock hit three in the afternoon. A small crooked table had been forgiven its handicap and covered with a lace doily and atop it, a fresh pot of tea in a white and red primrose teapot and an iced cake; proof that the women of the house had been there, although there were none to be seen any longer. The girls had been banished to their room. Only Hannah stood at the slit of the door, enabling the retelling of what happened next, for generations to come.

"So Mr Black, what brings you to our lovely town?" Father September began the conversation.

"Business Father. I have a small jewellery store in the city. Cape Jewellery Company, perhaps you have seen it?" replied Isaiah. His business had grown and flourished and had become well known.

"Why Mr Black, it is well respected. It is me who must now say I am complimented that a fine gentleman like you would come for tea in my house and pray in my church ... a European man like yourself." Father September sipped demurely from a cup of sweet, milky tea.

"I was born in Kimberley father."

"Oh, excuse the words of an ordinary man – I mean European in another sense." He sipped again.

"Well, it's not so much that I am European. My family, my mother is from Kimberley too."

"Oh I see. Did she move before or after the diamond rush?"

"She was born there too."

Father September shot Isaiah a confused look.

"Born in Kimberley? English?"

"No."

"Well then surely Afrikaner, Boer?"

"No."

"You don't mean ... ?" Father September stammered, panicked and, losing all sense of decorum, poured half of his tea into his saucer.

Isaiah sat quietly for a moment, again, weighing his fate.

"No, my mother was not European. My father was English, but not my mother."

"Speak up chap, what did you say?" Father September snapped like a tea biscuit.

"Her father was Xhosa and I think her mother was mixed, like you and I." He added hastily as he saw Father September's face climb to annoyance.

"Coloured, we prefer to say. We descend from the Europeans. Perhaps Asians. Not the blacks ... well, not really," Father September said fading off into his memory. "Anyway, that can't be avoided my boy, but if Mother finds out she will make life difficult for you. For both of us. This whole day she's been going on – 'A nice European man. The way he speaks, so well-dressed ...' on and on. Better you say nothing for now. Oh dash it." Father September, feeling suddenly quite relaxed, took a long slurp from his saucer as Isaiah sank into his chair.

The irony must have stung.

So then, to answer the question: was it love at first sight? For Hannah: yes, unequivocally. She had said so many times. And for Isaiah? Perhaps, Zara thought, Isaiah's union with Hannah was his stab at salvation.

9

The clouds were slipping off the mountain. Pouring down the sides, the greyness rolled its way toward the houses. It was the South Easter that brought these winds, and true to form it would blow for days and nights setting off car alarms one after the other, tree branches would wear scarves of plastic and women would find their dresses wrapped around their necks. From the *stoep* Zara watched the approaching wind. Her cousin Amy was cocooned in a hammock, reading something or other, her head always between those pages like a human bookmark. Amy had timed it all perfectly, lifting her hand whenever she wanted a page turned, and duly, the wind obliged. They were seventeen years old and had taken to spending the summer at their grandmother Hannah's house where they could escape the vigilance of their parents and other restrictions. Their ninety-two-year-old grandmother doted on them, preparing plates of sandwiches and her special recipe ginger beer all in exchange for their time, which the girls gave reluctantly, heady with their own youth.

"Wind's about to blow you apart, Amy," Zara shouted, walking into the folds of the house as the wind picked up speed and began to rattle the roof.

"Oh, really?" Amy said looking up after nearly a minute had passed. "Orright, coming inside." She unrolled herself from the hammock and hit the thick grass with a small thud.

When Zara opened her eyes it was still a shade of night outside. She could tell from where the white blinds snarled up in the corner. She burrowed into the covers for a few more minutes, the quilt up to her nose and her mind racing to remember her dreams before they faded. Since she had been here, in this foreign place, her dreams had taken on quixotic proportions and each night she wandered to new places recapturing events that had and had not occurred. All the people she had ever known, it seemed, were there too, waiting for her to fall back to sleep. But her most recent dream was about Amy, she remembered relieved. Not only her cousin, but her best friend.

Zara dressed quickly and ate an apple as she ventured out into the December snow. She would walk, she decided. She would walk to work in the very frostiness that had been the cause of so much misery all that week. Retail was down. The market was not bullish. Driveways were blocked. Roads were closed. Principals and super-intendents had discussed closing schools, but ultimately had not, prompting a second wave of unhappiness amongst students. Science and religion were in an arm wrestle – global climate change or the end of days? The weather channel meanwhile took a leap of faith and announced that it was now, officially, boot and sweater season. Ignoring all this, rivulets froze midstream while Zara walked to work. By the time she passed *Ortez and Sons*, she was beginning to regret her decision. Her face stung with the cold and she felt that her blood must have turned to slush. Even Mr Ortez had stayed indoors, only managing an insipid wave and a shoulder hunch that Zara gathered to mean, "Why are you out in this weather?" as she went by his store.

"Now most other people are taking the bus today, why you outside walking?" she heard from behind her as the campus shuttle bus slowed down, and she saw through the crack of the window a neat coil of braids piled high.

"It's cold, get inside here."

Zara would not turn down the offer. She had watched the campus bus passing by before but had never taken it, preferring the solitude of a cab on cold days. But today was no day to bother about privacy. She climbed aboard the bus, embarrassed to have been saved from herself mid-way on the journey to campus, but glad for the instant heat of the bus interior.

"Everyone's takin' a ride today, so you'll have to stand by my side," the bus driver added as Zara tried to gain her balance up front. "Humanities, right? I've seen you walking before."

"Yes, thank you, I don't know what I was thinking," Zara managed as her face started to regroup.

"*What were you thinking?* Today's no day to be out in this weather. And if this is December's attitude, then I don't wanna know January!" the woman said chuckling, her face breaking into a thousand soft lines.

"Yes, you're right. It just looked so beautiful outside. Where I'm from cold normally comes with dark skies and rain," Zara said, finding a place to rest her behind so that she would not topple over.

"Where are you from?" the woman inclined her whole head towards Zara.

"South Africa. And in Cape Town when it's cold, well, it looks cold ..."

"Yeah? I used to hear tons about South Africa on the news back in the day. Haven't heard anything in a while. I take it no news is good news?"

"Yes," Zara answered quietly.

"Now that is good news," the woman said, as she slowed down at a stop sign. "Can't take too much for granted nowadays. If the cold don't get you, and taxes don't, then it'll be something else alright. Then again, I'm healthy and I got my family. My boy," the driver pointed to a photograph pasted to the dashboard of a teenage boy. He was grinning back at his mother. "Seventeen next month and smart," she said, whistling between her teeth. "Wants to go to college. So what do I do? Send the boy to college, right? He can't kick or hit a ball to save himself," she chuckled again, "so I drive during the day, work another job at night and just keep prayin' that we get by when the time comes. We've got our health. Praise the Lord," she added.

"Yes, I know what you mean," Zara said, feeling lousy for having accepted a scholarship that she did not really want.

"You say Humanities? Here you go honey, you have a good day, alright?" the woman said, slowing the bus and shifting down so that she could stop outside Zara's building. "Now if you want a ride back you just stand right here. Every hour on the hour, alright?"

Zara said her thanks and made her way to her office. She did have her health. That was true. And Amy was family. So was Amy's mother, Aunty Rose. Not that there were many others. Zara had cousins, distant relatives and the like, but some were scattered around the world and those who were not only managed the occasional telephone call. Really, there were only Amy and Aunty Rose to count on in the way of Sunday lunch and Christmas gifts.

When Zara opened her email an hour later and saw the note from Amy, she knew that the conversation with the bus driver and her cousin's email would do what four layers of clothing and a cup of hot chocolate had not.

Zee, the email began, *finding your feet in freezing New Jersey?* Zara looked down at the black rubber snow boots she had found at a discount store, the tops of the furry white socks just visible beneath that and the ugly taupe stockings thankfully hidden beneath those. Her feet were there alright, she could hardly miss them.

Saw something on CNN about the cold. Well, we are having lovely weather. Reminds me of our endless summers at Ma Hannah's. By the way, when you planning to be back so we can do some summer stuff?

Zara read, and knew that this question was anything but by the way.

Her cousin had made it clear that she thought Zara should be home sorting out whether there was any validity to the government's claim, and helping to save the world as it seemed Amy, a doctor in a public hospital, was actually doing. As far as Zara could see, it took a special type of resilience to practise in the public service. She knew that Amy worked more than most, she sweated, she cursed, she fell down but got straight back up. As far as Zara was concerned, she was Amy the Amazing.

Not much happening here, Amy wrote.

In answer to your question: I've heard nothing about your dad. And doubt we will, Zee. Come home, at least to sort out whether there is anything to these claims. We knew your father and the idea that he did anything untoward is hard to believe. So maybe it's a case of mistaken identity or some crazy screw-up, don't you think?

Now, why the questions about our grandparents? I'll tell you what I know, though it won't be as much as you already know ... Ma Hannah was sixteen and Papa in his mid or late twenties when they met. Was it love at first sight? I don't know. Is it ever? Though during our summers with her, Ma Hannah always said it was. I'm sure you as family historian will know.

But all that belongs to another era. Let's put it behind us and then come home Zee, we miss you.

10

Zara's mind was on Isaiah.

How he must have kicked the dirt and scuffed his boots that Sunday as he walked home from the minister's house, having touched neither the cake nor his tea. After all, the conversation had been one-sided and the priest had talked local gossip, the gold rush, politics at the Cape – a place Isaiah had surely begun to understand was a lot more than it had first appeared. Losing all affectation, Father September had even begun to speak about the three girls and had conveniently confided to Isaiah that Hannah – not his daughter but his niece, he had emphasised – was of marrying age, having just turned sixteen.

"Should you take a fancy to my girl, you let me know," the minister had said, a wink hanging off his eye. "We'll keep your secrets between us, hey my boy?"

Isaiah left without saying another word.

Would he return the following Sunday and agree to disclose nothing of his conversation with the priest, accepting that his future lay not in what he could accomplish, but in the way he appeared?

He did not return to the church the next Sunday, nor ever again.

*

But of course, Zara's very presence was proof that matters were not left there. In her aging years it was this story that Hannah loved to repeat to an awed audience of two granddaughters, as she boasted how she too had been a liberated woman in her day.

"You pursued Papa?" came the shocked responses from Zara and Amy. Grandmothers were curious birds that were meant to conjure lovely things to eat, ooh and ahh over their grandchildren, have little else to do but attend to the family, and certainly, not chase men, even dead grandfathers.

As Hannah had it, having noticed Isaiah's absence from church, she turned up at his jewellery store one morning.

"You didn't come back?" Hannah began, twisting a bonnet mercilessly.

"I know. I'm sorry. I ..."

"Something about me? Or you changed your mind?" she asked, looking down.

"No. It isn't that. You see, I don't think I am quite what your family had in mind," Isaiah answered.

"But you want to court my family? I thought it was me you liked."

"I did ... I do. But sometimes life isn't that simple. Look, I'm not what I seem to be. You see?" Isaiah said, his head angled and his face softened.

"He isn't my father ... the minister, I mean," Hannah explained, lowering her voice. "Their permission would be nice, but I don't need it."

"Where are your parents?"

"They died four years ago. I was too young to look after myself. The minister and my aunty even think I am inferior to them. They thought my father was the wrong man for my mother: too dark; too much like a Bushman. They are my family and I am thankful, but I don't see everything the way they do."

"Do they treat you badly?"

"I'm not Cinderella," Hannah said, stifling a giggle. "If you want to court me, you have my blessing."

"I do Hannah, I really do," said Isaiah, bewitched at the young girl's quiet smile.

*

Hannah had left the small Karoo town where she'd been born, days after she had lost her parents in a fire that had burnt their home down to the veined earth, her parents still inside. The Karoo reverend and his young Cape wife had been posted to the town to run the parish for one of the town's two churches. The town had two congregations: the Afrikaners, and whomever else remained. It was in the latter church that Hannah's father was a priest. An "ungodly and unkind place," the young married woman, Hannah's mother, had famously said when she'd first put her bags down and tried to imagine a life there, but Hannah grew up knowing nothing else and craved what her mother hated: hot, dry air on her face, sand beneath her toes, the sound of cicadas all through the day and night and people who greeted whether they knew her or not, though everyone knew everyone else in that place.

For her remaining days Hannah thought of *that* Karoo town as home and still awoke with her legs tingling with the brush of grass that had scratched at her knees as a girl. She said that she continued to think about the two gravestones, overgrown and dirty from not being visited. She thought about them every day.

Hannah had already left for school when it happened. A candle must have fallen over and by the time Hannah arrived back home, nothing remained of the small wooden house. Her parents: both dead and an entire world reduced to a heap of embers. She had no one left and nothing. For days she'd cried and found some solace in the kindness of people who lived in the small town, but she couldn't stay. People were poor and she was just one more stomach, so she'd left for Cape Town with borrowed money, a hat and pair of gloves donated from the Dominee's wife (the reverend's spouse from the blessed side of town had sent over a parcel of food and clothes). Her eyes finally dried and her resolve set, Hannah left the Karoo days after her unacknowledged twelfth birthday.

She thought that she would never have a home again, and yet, along had come Isaiah.

*

Hannah and Isaiah built their house on a hill with the ocean before them and the mountain at their back.

For their marriage and life together there was plenty of evidence: wedding pictures faded by time, a wedding dress grown yellow, the acrid smell of moth balls lingering in Zara's memory. Their children: Martha, Jean, Emma, Rose, Bart, and, the children's children in turn. And then, of course, there was the house.

Hannah learnt Isaiah's tastes for the expensive early and as Zara could recall, days might be spent deciding the perfect colour of a lampshade or the design of a teacup. What Zara knew of Hannah was intimately entwined with the house. In fact, she realised she could not imagine Hannah apart from it at all. They were a single entity. It was Isaiah's sense of precision that ruled inside and the order of the family home began with a kitchen where everything worked on schedule and where everything had its place: from the smallest of teaspoons to pots and pans placed in ascending order.

Doors were always open, so light rolled off the white walls, and at night the house was closed behind damask curtains in shades of red and copper. Cushions were spread on chairs, while rugs covered wooden floors, and where there was not an object of beauty, nature was tamed into bunches of flowers.

While the inside of the house remained defined by Isaiah, it was the garden where Hannah ruled. Outside was wild and carefree. The front garden was filled with rose bushes, rows of lavender encircled the house, filling the air with their pungent scent, bougainvilleas clung to the walls and fruit trees held off the sun.

It was the garden which Zara yearned for that night and often thereafter, in those cold months of the New Jersey winter.

II

As the woman unfurled a crumpled note, the American flag painted on nails that arched over the tips of her fingers, Zara had this question: what was the thing lodged between longing and loathing? That sensation she could feel pressing against her diaphragm that made her despise, even if just a little, all that she missed – her father, her country and even her beloved mother.

The ticket seller pushed Zara's change through the glass mouth of the booth and mumbled something beneath her breath; it might have been have a nice day. Zara passed over the woman's irritation. It wasn't bad for a Sunday morning in the heart of winter. After the onset of snow, winter had receded and settled into a bearable chill, so perhaps she had better places to be than the train station, the smell of urine bubbling up between heavy doses of pine-scented disinfectant.

The early train to New York City was cramped and Zara sculpted herself into the space alongside the window at the back of the carriage. Talkative children pointed outside, teenagers spoke loudly on their cell phones and displaced lovers dozed against the windows of New Jersey Transit – the wires that reached into their ears and blocked the clamour of the day, transported them to other places yet, perhaps even back into the arms of those they had left behind.

It was Zara's day off and the rich morning air had lured her out of her apartment and onto a train headed for the city. She would walk to one of the galleries, maybe MOMA, then browse around a book store, find something to eat and then she would take the train back to her single room, the place where silence was not only leaving its mark on her but where she was learning the many grades of quiet that existed in her world. Aside from that, there was no place to move because her apartment was covered in batches of paper. She had cluttered the white one-roomed flat with her signature mess. All over the room books and manuscripts abounded; only the single bed remained free.

Zara watched the suburbs give way to the muscular sprawl of suspended bridges, tire factories, apartment blocks and train stations that became more decrepit as Manhattan approached, and when Zara had settled into this mindless gazing, the day's newspaper unread on her lap, she felt the compartment's double seat depress. Someone had sat down beside her, was now looking at her, closely.

"I ride the trains," a man's voice said.

Zara looked at him briefly, turned back to the window. She had been warned about people on trains here.

"I ride the trains most days," the stranger persisted. "You never know who you will meet. Like you, who knew I would meet you today?" he said, and waited.

"Yes, hi, thank you," Zara said, glimpsing the man's fading black suit jacket turned in at the collar and his grizzly unshaven face, before she returned to the window. She did not want to have a conversation with him.

"I can't pinpoint your accent, where are you from?" he asked politely, so that Zara strained to remain quiet.

"South Africa" she answered after a moment, the man's stare digging into her, before she looked around self-consciously to see if anyone was watching. No one was.

"South Africa? Oh. I was married to an African-American woman once. Well, if you apply the term married loosely," he said, folding his hands comfortably before him.

Zara feigned great interest in a gnarled tree outside, its whorled bark wrapped around part of a building.

"Now, you don't read too much about your country. Always the good ol' U.S. of A ... if it's not our celebrities, it's our wars and if it's not that it's the price of gas ..."

Zara opened the paper and began to skim through the pages.

"You know, we have an African-American man running for the presidency, did you know?" He bent in close, Zara caught a whiff of soap, like the heavy block sort that was used to wash clothes or dishes at home.

"No, I did not, really?" Zara replied, annoyed that she had been distracted from her idle city watching.

"Ah, a joke? Yes, you're having me on. You read. Probably read lots about everything. I can tell. Always can. It's in the eyes: intelligence. Window to the soul, typa thing. And where the brain resides. Dull eyes, well, no bright ideas taking place, no fusion of connectors. It was a joke right?"

"Well, I was being sarcastic ... and yes, I know who the candidates are," Zara said, softening. "Why do you want to speak to me? I have nothing to say, and no one speaks on the train here anyway," Zara said exasperated, and pointed around for emphasis.

"That's exactly why. See, I'm a contrarian. Do my best work swimming against the tide." He wove his hand, fishlike, through the air in demonstration. "In the sixties when everyone else was sleeping around, listening to Bob Dylan, I was celibate, listened to native Rain Forest music ..."

"I thought Bob Dylan was *the* contrarian?"

"Well, *he* was, but everyone listening to him ... I'm not so sure about them."

"And then you married an African-American woman?"

"Yes, but not to be different. I fell in love, but we never did get married, not in the eyes of the law at least. We stayed together all of ten years, till she decided she had enough of me. Said I was impossible ..." he was saying, relaxing into the conversation when the ticket inspector who had been edging closer, stopped at their seat.

"Oh, gimme a break!" the woman began irritably, her khaki uniform straining threateningly at the two middle buttons on her shirt. "Why you have to be on my train? There's a train every ten minutes in every direction in this state and you always pick mine?" she said, and placed a hand on her hip for emphasis.

"Because I missed your wit and charm ..." the man replied, returning her stare cautiously.

"Next station!"

"Actually, you see, actually today I was planning on going all the way to Manhattan. Train to Connecticut leaves at twelve," he replied politely, and anxiously checked the empty space on his arm where a watch had once been.

"Unless you can pay, you're getting out at the next stop, my friend."

The man scratched about in his pocket, his bag, came up five dollars short.

"Right then, next station."

"Wait," Zara said, and reaching into her bag extracted five dollars.

"Well, it's your money ..." grumbled the inspector, her hand reluctantly accepting the coins, before she wrote out a ticket.

"You see, you never know who you'll meet on a train," the man said, as the ticket officer walked away shaking her head, before he turned to Zara and added kindly, "That was real nice of you."

"No trouble." Zara did not know why she had done that. Perhaps because it was the first conversation she had had in a long while or, like at home, she never could turn away. In some South African cities, one rarely passed a major traffic intersection without encountering boys, some as young as twelve cleaning car windows between the changing traffic lights for a R2 coin. Nor could one walk down a busy main road without giving to someone who needed an odd for a loaf of bread.

"So, why do you ride the trains?" Zara asked after she had taken out a map in order to decide where she would walk.

"Why not ride the trains?"

"Yes, I see your point ..."

"I observe. Sometimes I even par-ti-ci-pate. Yes, you see some days maybe someone needs to talk. Maybe this person has no one to speak to, or, no one to listen to them ... it's amazing how many people in the world feel all alone ... and so yours truly has found a niche ..."

"Like a therapist?" Zara enquired, looking at the man closely: his eyes burning bright, his broad nose twitching when he said certain words.

"More like a barman, minus the booze, I'd say," he said, pouring an invisible drink into an invisible glass in his hand, "... and some days you meet someone who is just waiting for a bit of advice ... like you ..." he added, taking a sip.

"Oh, really? What sort of advice?"

"You're going to a notoriously aggressive city with a map in your hand ... not a good idea. They won't give you the time of day that way. No, not New Yorkers. And don't ask directions either, shows weakness. Also never apologise. People will think you're soft, and never hesitate when you cross a street, New Yorkers never do, you'll get killed that way ... just take the city like you own it, the rest will follow ..."

"Those certainly are a lot of rules ..."

"No, not rules. Skills that no one ever tells you, but things which you gotta know," he said, with great confidence. "Like don't blow your nose into a single piece of tissue paper, no, you gotta double it. And don't eat the napkin around the hotdog," he added, "gives you indigestion."

"I'll try to remember," Zara said, laughing openly as the train pulled into the station, and people started shuffling towards the exit.

The stranger stood, delivered a half bow as he thanked Zara again for her kindness, wished her a wonderful life and rushed to catch his next train.

*

Exiting the train station, Zara made her way into the ubiquitous clamour of Seventh Avenue. She slipped into a stream of pedestrian traffic moving down the pavement and stayed behind a set of broad, anonymous shoulders until she could break free and turn down one of the side streets. It was a day for sitting outside, so she stopped at a nearby park, found herself a cup of coffee and watched a chess game in progress.

To her left Zara watched a family taking pictures on the lawn beyond the sign that read, *No Walking on the Grass*. The collective had tried all conceivable ways of getting everyone into the picture, but finally exhausted by missing the click of the camera poised on a tree trunk, they turned around frustrated and found Zara watching them.

"Could you take a picture of us? There's ten of us and heck, we all want to be in it!" the elderly woman said, looking accusingly at the large family.

"Certainly. You should move closer though. Closer. Good," Zara said, and through the lens saw the family's trajectory from grandmother, through her children, to the toddlers trying to climb trees and ruining their neat Sunday clothes.

Zara's own family was also just starting to come into focus since she had started shaking the family tree, comparing stories that she and her cousin Amy had been told, interrogating family legends for inconsistencies. She had emailed Amy a series of questions, and Zara went so far as to include her ageing Aunty Rose (her father's sister and Amy's mother) in her research, hoping that this might unseat long held family myths. Rose had taken to Zara's excavation of the family past with gusto, replying in long letters and posting these every week or two. Zara had received one such letter that morning.

Rose was the youngest of her father's four sisters and one of only two of that generation of the Black clan still living. Rose: named for the loveliest of flowers by her father, and who insisted on living alone in the yellow and white house that fell somewhere behind the mountain. Still, it was the only house she had ever shared with her long dead husband. Rose: who survived on a diet of daily soaps and who had always, of the Black siblings, been the least liked.

When Rose had first heard that Zara was leaving she had exclaimed with delight.

"Oh, wonderful! Better somewhere else, what with all that's happening here, now just convince your cousin to go too," she'd said.

This had become the conversation around which all family meals and gatherings started to rotate and whirl out of control. Aunty Rose seemed to have an ever growing mental file of what was wrong with the country and therefore who was leaving and who was speaking about leaving. "Even that activist that you two respect, that one that sat on Robben Island for ten years. Guess where he is now? America. And your cousin, Petra, with that good for nothing husband who only gets out of his pyjamas to take a shower ... New Zealand, they leave next week ..."

"Yes, Mom. But let's not have this conversation again today, alright? Zara is not leaving for that reason. And anyway, we should leave and go where?" Amy had asked rhetorically.

"But you're a doctor Amy, you could go anywhere. Somewhere with lovely hospitals. Without worries over being stuck with a needle full of AIDS, no rape victims for you to have nightmares about, no incompetent hospital management. Nice old dying people, cancer victims, brain tumours and so on," Aunty Rose had said to her only daughter, who regarded her with a look of disbelief.

"Perhaps I should filter what I tell you about work in future. And anyway – who on earth will put up with you if I don't?"

At that Rose had skulked around Amy's flat for the rest of the afternoon, only resuming any sort of conversation on the drive home with Zara.

"You know, I say these things so she will understand, Zara. And you too. You girls must understand. I mean. You know, what must we think? All this violence and crime? You can say what you like about all people being the same and equal, but my goodness, it wasn't like this before."

Zara should have intervened, should have told her to shut up. Nothing less would have done. Instead, Zara had turned away and wondered at the shade of sunset.

"I mean, gosh, when we were young, oh, we could walk all the way from one side of town to the other without anyone interfering with us. And if the *skollies* did interfere it was just to say good evening and how nice we looked. But now, look at the country. It's not that I didn't want them to have their freedom. It's what they've done with it, Zara ..." Aunty Rose had continued, her voice tilting towards feverish with every new word.

"Aunty Rose, you weren't free either, then," Zara said quietly, as they moved along the highway in slow motion.

Aunty Rose had continued, unabated.

"Oh, things were different then. There wasn't AIDS and corruption. And you know, yes, I do admire the Europeans, and why not with all they've done for the country? And the blacks can't very well keep blaming apartheid. Of course, I wasn't allowed to say this to your father. No. He said I was a racialist. But now, look, *they* say *he* is a traitor."

"Look Aunty Rose, I don't want to hear this. I really don't. Your opinions do you no favours, not with me, and definitely not Amy ... everything is so, well, black and white for you when I think you know life is far more complex ..." Zara had begun, but realised how futile any argument was with Aunty Rose, especially when she had made up her mind. So she'd changed tack instead.

"... Good grief, look a rainbow, in the middle of this downpour," Zara had said, pointing somewhere, anywhere, out of the car. Rose had continued, and so they drove home, Zara trying to deflect Aunty Rose's attention towards the shade of the mountain at that hour, or the fact that she saw flowers even in that downpour of cold June, or to enquire whether some distant relative might be having a birthday soon. But somehow, no matter how Zara had tried, Aunty Rose always did make her point.

Zara breathed in deeply, tore open the letter from Aunty Rose and skimmed the contents. Her aunt had written in a frail, but neat cursive:

*My father tried his best. Of course he didn't want to be ashamed
of his mother, but he had been educated and you know, she didn't
have a day of school. It was the only way he could advance
in life, to leave his mother behind, I mean. As for your father:
I don't believe this traitor nonsense. Say what you like, he was
strange, always was. But a traitor? I can't believe. Probably, this
is just government shenanigans! But he never spoke to me about
those things. He and I could never agree about politics. I didn't
like the people he sometimes got involved with. So that was that.
And anyway Zara, you should just put all of this behind you.
Forget the letter. Start again.*

12

But there could be no forgetting that letter. On the day of its arrival, Zara, hands trembling, called her cousin Amy. She was always careful about disturbing Amy in the middle of the day. In the hospital where Amy worked, resources were often scarce, services sometimes went undelivered, and queues of injured and sick sat on long wooden benches for hours until a doctor could see them. Zara knew Amy's daily encounters were beyond her own imagining, but her cousin answered the phone quickly that day.

"Amy, can you talk?"

"Give me a minute. Just hold on," Amy said, and Zara could hear her shoes clacking against linoleum floors. "Zee. What's up?" Amy spoke breathlessly.

"So ... I just received this letter. Out of the blue ... no, it's not a letter. An official notification from the government. Amy, it says that my father was involved in something ..." she exhaled loudly: "A betrayal of sorts. They say the details will only be released in time to come. I don't know what to make of it ..."

"What? That's bizarre. Zee, wait one minute ..." and she was off shouting at someone in the background about wiping up a mess.

"Zee, what is the point of the letter?" Amy returned, a new urgency in her voice.

"It seems to be saying ... the implication is that he was part of something sinister."

"Something sinister?"

"Like maybe ..." Zara paused a moment too long, "... he was an informer or a spy ... God, I don't know Amy."

"That can't be true. Your father was a decent, honest man, and the only person in the entire family who gave a damn about what was happening beyond the walls of that house on the hill. Where are they getting this from?"

"I don't know – documents that were previously classified or something like that ..."

"Shit. Listen Zee, something is going down here. I have to go, but I'll call you after work. Will you be fine until then?"

"Of course I will. Of course," she said, before hanging up.

Later that day Zara drove to the family home, the letter still clutched in her hand.

That house was a law unto itself. Neither human nor animal, but spirit all the same, a monolith of white stone that rose high against the day, glinting in the sun. Perhaps the house had been Isaiah's most definitive message to the world. Still, it had always had some power over Zara, so she was drawn back there when she was at a loss and needed something – quiet or calm or to feel the presence of family. With the weight of all its memories, to Zara, the house felt like family. She paused on top of the hill, stopped at the gate and hooted so that the watchman came out. Bending low, the man saw that it was her.

"*Molo siesie*," he said, wiping a line of sweat away with the back of his arm. It was sweltering. "You coming to visit?" he asked, smiling widely. He was accustomed to her occasional visits when she wanted to find something amongst her father's things, or just sit in the garden for a few minutes so that she could remember her mother. It was here that her mother Lena had eventually come to live, or rather, come to die. They had moved into the house two years before Lena's death; for Zara, it had been perhaps the happiest time of her life.

Then, after her father's death, the house, with the exception of one storeroom, had been donated to a local organisation to use as offices. The house was too big and too much for one person to be concerned about – her grandmother's roses after all those years still battling the odds, defying Cape Town's tender days and then sudden mood swings.

Zara drove up the short pathway, between the fruit trees, and noticed that they were slowly being coaxed back to life after years of neglect when Bart had lived there. She found a shady spot to park her car and went to the back of the house, where her father's things were kept. The room still carried Bart's scent: books, shoe polish, the inside of kitchen cupboards. No soap-on-a-rope or Old Spice, like that of other fathers. No, there had always just been him, Bart: clean and polished and studious.

The evening light angled its way through the slit of the door. Zara swore beneath her breath.

"Shit."

And then a little louder. "Shit!"

He had been a nice man. Everyone had said so at his funeral. And that was the truth. He *had* been nice. A decent man. Often kind. Certainly not selfish. But what no one had said as they gathered to say their final goodbyes was how deflated Bart had been. The look in his eye that showed his disappointment at life, the way some men twinkled at the sight of a bit of naked leg or others smirked at someone's misfortunes. It had been there, embedded in his face: had it not been for his far younger wife and daughter, he would simply have let go and floated away.

Perhaps Zara finally knew why.

She walked to the neatly labelled shelves and tipped her father's books to the floor. She riffled through pages and turned each book upside down with the sort of irreverence which she had been taught never to show books, gripped by a rising anger at the silent dead: her parents who, even in this labyrinthine mystery, had only left questions. She searched amongst her father's books for something, a clue, a bit of paper, any kind of explanation.

She stayed that way for an hour until she stumbled across her father's collection of music. His albums were still in pristine condition, and, taking a few of his more recent discs, she left his books strewn across the floor and locked the door behind her. Zara looked at the old house one last time, turned to wave at the guard, and drove through the gate and away.

13

Thelonious Monk's *Round Midnight*. Or was this the Miles Davis version? Zara did not know. This was the music of another generation, not her own, not even her mother's. Zara only remembered that she had brought some of her father's music with her when the discord of traffic and snatches of hip hop from the street below snuck into her room on Bloomfield Avenue and left her desperate for a diversion.

For as long as she could recall, her father had collected long playing records, and when those started to vanish, he begrudgingly bought cassettes, until finally he succumbed, reluctantly, to CDs. Somewhere between losing his will to practice law and becoming an English teacher, he had found a love of jazz. Zara could remember him seated in the lounge, eyes closed, giving the appearance of *any* old man napping in the middle of the day aside from the tapping of his forefinger against his thigh.

In contrast, her mother's music was folksy, inherently feminine. Joan Baez, Bread, Carol King, and then there were the Marley years, music that Zara had pinned to her mother's very existence. Did she really listen to any of it? Or wear long skirts and tie-dyed sweaters? And did bursts of patchouli really fill the room as her mother walked by, after all? This was how Lena was remembered: all seventies even in the eighties, and having found her era, she stuck to it resolutely.

Like the men Zara noted sitting outside their stores on the sidewalks of Bloomfield Avenue speaking Spanish, their handlebar moustaches and white hats a distant call to another land, another time.

Zara stopped the music abruptly. She did not want to hear anything that her father had once loved. Still, the reconstruction of her father's life had begun in earnest, and what was there to say about it?

Perhaps, that he had been called Bartholomew Isaiah Howard Black, a Christian name for every patriarch in the family: one from his own father Isaiah, his mother's deceased father Howard, and then of course a name for himself: Bartholomew, the name shortened to Bart by sisters who did not have the patience for syllables. His birth date: 3 April 1935, ten years behind the last girl born to the Black family.

By the time Bart met Zara's mother, Lena, he was already in his forties. So when Zara was born he was the oldest father around. It was an era when the older parent was still an anomaly, when it was scarcely trendy to be one. He had loved to listen to jazz. He had taught English to students who preferred the writings of revolutionaries to the school's prescribed list. They wanted to read detractors and rebels of any sort: Wally Serote, Athol Fugard, Ellison, Neruda, Gordimer. He had taught a riotous generation that would try to unseat the government one day.

Beyond this, what did Zara know?

In reclaiming the past, Bart's sister Rose had a contribution to make. What must her aunty's life be like, Zara wondered? Living alone, with only her routine and the regularity of her neighbours passing by on their way elsewhere to keep her anchored.

Most likely, for Aunty Rose, the letters were a pleasant distraction from the drudgery of days that formed one long arc from morning to night. What was to be done after breakfast was eaten, phone calls made and daily soapies watched? Certainly, she could probably have another meal and start the whole process again and so on until the day was done and she and Amy finally spoke on the telephone (as they did every evening, Zara knew). Perhaps, the letters kept her occupied, and new correspondence had arrived once again that morning.

Aunty Rose's letter, as always, was filled with news from home: someone whom Zara did not know had died, someone else had gotten married, Zara read, skipping over the horror stories and complaints she was always hearing from her aunt. Finally, her aunt's thoughts about home purged, Rose continued to the reason for her letter.

After a life of secrets, their father Isaiah had finally told them everything about his past, one Sunday afternoon.

I will never forget that day. It took his last bit of energy.
Perhaps if Daddy hadn't made the confession – his peace, Bart
called it – perhaps he would have held on for a few more months.
He gathered us all together and he told us everything: about
the diamonds, yes. But that he never went back for his mother
upset Daddy most.

He said he decided to tell us so we could finally know him.
Until then we had not even known our grandmother's name:
Martha, like our sister.

The truth, though, is that I was not devastated by these revelations. None of us girls were. Yes, it was a scandal not to be spoken about, of course. But we had never known our grandmother, and Daddy had been a loving father, so it was his pain that we felt. And as for passing as white – well, you can ask any coloured family, everyone knows one person who disappeared to the other side, often never to be heard of again. So that was nothing new.

Bart, though, he became angry, stormed out of the house and only returned a week later. He was upset about the betrayal of a grandmother no one knew. He was upset about the secrets of all those years. Not that stolen diamonds had made our family's fortune, but that secrets and lies had. He was upset about everything. I think something changed in your father after that. Though, to be honest, your father always was a bit strange.

14

Thing is, the whole Black family was an odd bunch with unusual occupations, but what could you expect from a house full of women (Bart had, perhaps teasingly, told Zara).

By the time Bart was born, Isaiah and Hannah's family was already in full swing: Martha, Jean, Emma and Rose had grown into young ladies (as they liked to refer to themselves when they were too old to recall having been anything else), preternaturally lovely in their burgeoning womanhood – *if* the family record was to be believed. When Bart showed up a decade behind the last girl, he was a lone boy, fighting for space and his father's attention. This was what Zara knew of her father's boyhood: that he was caught somewhere between sisters who lavished attention on him or ignored him entirely, and a father who may have been dedicated to his girls, but who had grown weary of child rearing by the time Bart arrived.

Bart too had come into Isaiah and Hannah's world late in their lives, the accidental last child who was adored and overprotected. Hannah was forty, while Isaiah was a decade ahead of her, an old man by then, Zara's father had said. Bart's four sisters meanwhile had graduated from girls on a mission to dig up Hannah's garden, into teenagers: there was Martha the tearful, who could sob for hours at an indirect slight; Emma, who despite the fact that she had fiercely talkative sisters, or perhaps because of it, preferred her own company; Jean, with the mammoth heart and who was best loved by everyone; and finally Rose, who seemed to have spent an entire youth worrying about shades of lipstick. All the girls were mad for their father, while Hannah and Bart had their own world. Hannah doted on her only son, reserving a look only for him. His birthday never escaped her, even though Hannah was wont to forget any of her girls' birthdays if not reminded. In fact, Zara herself had a special place carved into Hannah's life because she was born of that boy child.

That partiality, for which Zara had no comparison being an only child, struck her many years later. There was a picture Zara could recall having seen: against the backdrop of Hannah's garden, a boy dangled off the edge of his mother's legs. The inscription behind the photograph, in Hannah's tight sparse handwriting, read: *summer 1940*.

Zara knew that something had happened in that garden, maybe during the summer of 1940. There were varying accounts of what precisely had taken place and how it had all played out, but that something had occurred was not disputed by any one of the Black siblings, nor that it was this that had nudged Bart down the path away from his father.

*

There was an unseasonal downpour during a Cape Town summer. That is how the story began.

Still, the garden must have worn its loveliness in the overlapping bougainvilleas, Frangipani trees dropping white and yellow blossoms, and an orchard of fruit trees.

It was late November, school had closed for the year and the girls in the family had decided to host readings of their favourite books in the garden, inviting their neighbours over to join them. Many of those who were invited arrived, not so much for the readings, as Zara could surmise so many years later, but because it was the only house on the street where fruit could be picked from the trees and where pots of tea made their way around the crowd while home-baked cakes were offered by the lovely Black sisters.

"We were cultured ..." Rose insisted, about those days.

"The rest of the country was struggling, defying government regulations and you lot were reading in the garden, gazing north ..." Amy demurred sulkily.

"And I suppose you think the whole country was always suffering. Even the oppressed laughed! And we brought brightness to those spinsters' lives ... and your Aunty Jean married an Adams boy – that was how they met ..."

Yes, the Adams boys, seven to be exact, who apparently never otherwise had the pleasure of finishing a slice of cake each, what with having to share beds, and clothes and even shoes. And of course, the three retired sisters from across the road, not a married one amongst them, who swore they came only for the reading, but never turned down a good Victoria Sponge and a cup of tea either.

Once everyone was seated – kitchen chairs for grownups and blankets that absorbed the last of the damp from the earth for children, one of the Adams boys began to read *Pride and Prejudice*. The teenage Black sisters had declared themselves Anglophiles that very summer, and anyway, they were reading Austen at school.

Bart took his place on his mother's lap as Aldous Adams (future uncle to Zara) stood before the crowd and cleared his voice in preparation for his debut performance.

The story had reached a critical point: Elizabeth was about to be proposed to by her cousin, and the Black sisters, romantics all, were desperate to know what would happen next. Aldous began to read; his moment to impress Jean Black had arrived.

On finding Mrs Bennet, Elizabeth, and one of the younger girls together, soon after breakfast, he addressed the mother in these words, "May, I hope, Madam, for your interest with your fair daughter Elizabeth, when I solicit the honour of a private audience with her in the course of this morning?"

Before Elizabeth had time for anything but a blush of surprise, Mrs Bennet instantly answered,

"Oh dear! – Yes – certainly. — I am sure Lizzy will be very happy – I am sure she can have no objection. – Come, Kitty. I want you upstairs." And gathering her work together, she was hastening away, when Elizabeth called out, "Dear Ma'am, do not go. – I beg you will not go.—Mr Collins must excuse me. —He can have nothing to say to me that anybody need not hear. I am going away myself.

"No, no, nonsense, Lizzy. — I desire you will stay where you are."

And upon Elizabeth's seeming really, with vexed and embarrassed looks, about to escape, she added, "Lizzy, I insist upon your staying and hearing Mr Collins."

It was Bart, facing the crowd, who first saw the woman. She was long and slender, and her arms pushed open the gate. Dry wood brushing against metal sounded, as the gate opened and drowned out Aldous' voice, crackling like a live radio transmission. Everyone turned to see who had arrived late, but the woman paid them no attention. Without looking at anyone, she strolled slowly through the garden and found an empty chair at the front of the yard.

The short black ringlets that framed the woman's face suggested a movie star, and her blue eyes, visible even in the demi-light, lit her face from within as they stared straight ahead of her. The ruffles of her cream blouse rose and fell as she positioned herself on a chair; the plum fabric of her skirt stopped dangerously just below her knee. With care the stranger removed just one glove; her hand revealing a hexagonal sapphire.

She smiled deliciously at Aldous to resume. Aldous continued, glad that this interruption was over, his voice growing steadier and more confident until he was drifting dreamily through the chapter. Few had continued to listen. Some wondered who the stranger was. "She must be from another city," it was determined in unspoken consensus; others continued to question what she was doing there, in the ordinary surroundings of their summer readings. Only Hannah no longer speculated.

Bart watched his mother unable to take her eyes from the woman while the stranger sat seemingly unaware of the unease her presence had provoked.

As soon as Aldous reached the end of the chapter, Martha and Jean jumped up, ready to thank the lady for having come, but she was already exiting through the gate and walking quickly down the hill.

*

Bart recalled the gloom coming off his mother in waves of disquiet for weeks after the stranger's visit to the summer reading; it was an ache he would attribute to his father, for reasons that he then couldn't understand.

Bart told Zara that after that, Hannah changed. He never elected to defend his father's reputation, and anyway, the affair, as it came to be known, might have been a secret once, but like other families, the Blacks could not prevent a rumour that started somewhere at the top making its way down the ranks, even to helpless children.

Bart said Hannah's usual hours spent tinkering in her garden were reduced to minutes avoiding rain, insects and all sorts of perils she had never otherwise noticed. That was also the summer that Hannah returned to the church.

It would take Bart many years to realise what had happened that summer, and by the time he was old enough to ask questions, he already knew the answers. For Bart, summer and childhood had both come to an abrupt end.

About the woman, family consensus was shaky. That a beautiful stranger had appeared was not disputed. That she had been Isaiah's lover was never openly acknowledged, least of all by Hannah who denied the woman right out of existence. No such thing had occurred and she was therefore never to be mentioned.

Still, everyone knew. The hexagonal ring, after all, had been chosen by Hannah for the store.

When Bart saw the same face many years later at his father's funeral, hanging behind the crowd, solemnly watching the family, it was all the confirmation he had ever needed.

*

Zara reckoned she understood, as she prepared to go to bed that night, what had drawn the battle line between her father and grandfather.

15

Zara pressed a shirt, pulled on a pair of jeans, and readied herself for the brunch in the city with her new colleague. The woman with whom she now shared the small office had arrived one week earlier, three months later than expected, carrying coffee and a leather bag slung over her shoulder.

"I'm Ling," she had said politely but in a matter-of-fact tone, as her scent – a light fragrance, perhaps of blossoms or summer fruit – filled the small office. "Is this my place?" she'd asked, and without waiting for an answer had settled into the empty desk.

Ling wasn't a local, Zara had decided after a few furtive glances. Her groomed appearance didn't complement the awkward New Jersey institution. Zara liked the University of Berwick. It was considered solid with a good reputation, often referred to as unpretentious – really another way of saying it wasn't the kind of Ivy League institution where you went if your family had money. Unlike Zara and her misfit colleagues who had no doubt gravitated to the campus for a quiet, if not invisible place in academia, her new colleague didn't seem the usual type to hang around a place like this. And the bag – Zara could have sworn it was the same one she had seen while flipping through a magazine in the doctor's office; it neared the price of college tuition.

"The bag was a gift from my mother," Ling had said, as she caught Zara in her peripheral vision, still staring. "I thought it would be wasteful not to use it since it had already been bought."

"Excuse me? I'm sorry, I recognised it from a magazine," Zara had replied embarrassed, trying not to gawk at the crocodile skin bag, adding "It's, well, interesting," by way of an apology.

"You think? My mother bought it for me and quite frankly I thought it was disgusting. But she's my mother, you know? She seems to get some sort of motherly payback when I actually appreciate her gifts."

"What are you working on?" Zara had asked, in an uncharacteristic effort at outreach, before adding, "I'm doing a paper on Mali's ancient scrolls."

"Oh I'm just here for two semesters to teach a first year seminar: 'Chairman Mao and the Cultural Revolution' – part of the China course," Ling had answered, dispirited.

"You'd rather be elsewhere?"

"History wasn't my decision at all. My father wanted me to study medicine, or law, or go into business, bit of a cliché. Something either with prestige or money, but unfortunately I didn't show sufficient intellectual curiosity. One thing led to another and I ended up studying history as a compromise," she'd said in one breath, as her fingers fluttered across her keyboard. "Where are you from?"

"South Africa. You?"

"Here, there, mostly New York of late. Moved to the States when I was twelve. You like it here?" Ling had continued, still not looking up from what she was doing.

"Some days ..." Zara had answered, but began shuffling papers so that Ling would get the message that it was time to get back to work.

"Jersey is a bit drab though, quite sad in some places. I could never live here. Never," she'd declared dramatically. "It's too ... too in between. Give me New York or Shanghai or Mumbai." She'd paused, "... Some place on the edge, curious, dangerous even. Anyway, I guess some people like it, they live here don't they?" Ling had asked, as she began shutting down her lap top. "Ok, that's enough work for one day, can I buy you lunch? You look hungry," she'd said, appraising Zara closely.

*

It had been impossible not to befriend Ling, Zara thought as she gathered up her things and began the journey to Manhattan for the brunch to which Ling had invited her. She couldn't help but be intrigued by her colleague. In another time and place, she might have found Ling's tardiness annoying, her aimlessness frustrating or her wealthy accessories part of another world, but instead, Zara began to look forward to Ling's arrival each morning in the office. Besides, it had been a long time since Zara had traded banter with someone and she found Ling's stories and anecdotes about her socialite mother and father, who had opened a chain of restaurants across the US, a distraction from the intricacies of her own life.

Zara braved New Jersey Transit and at the other end of the journey queued in line for a cab.

"So where you from?" the taxi driver asked. She usually encountered this desire for human connection between those from outside of America on her trips to the City.

"I'm from Calcutta," he said, moving in for a closer look in the rear view mirror, an air of flirtation clouding his view of her. "So tell me please, where you from? You not Indian girl, no ... Egyptian maybe? You look to me like you could be Egyptian princess even," he said, revving the engine, his eyes fixed on her reflection as New York City cabs droned past.

"I'm South African," Zara smiled politely and looked out of the window.

"South Africa? Lots of Indians there. I hear lots of Indians and lovely girls," he added shyly, his head bobbing now to a rhythm that he had turned up on the car radio.

"Yes, one of the biggest Indian diasporas – people from India living elsewhere – in the world," she said.

"Yes, thank you very much, I'm medical student, I know what diaspora means. I just drive taxis for now. One day I can practice medicine again," said the taxi driver, his glossy black hair swaying gently from side to side, an indication that he would not offend her in turn. "But what are you ... please?"

"I told you, I'm South African."

"Yes, but you not look very black and of course also not white."

Zara did not reply, but looked out of the window at the passing traffic on Sixth Avenue, wondering about this human preoccupation with bloodlines and the need to ascribe place and identity to each other.

"Excuse me, you not answer me," the taxi driver repeated, his head swaying even more.

"Me? Probably everything," Zara answered beneath a loud sigh, resigned that the man would have his answer.

"What you say?" he inclined his head towards her.

"African, Asian and European. A little of each," she answered, annoyed that she had not told him to mind his own business.

"African? Oh ..." he said, surprised and sad all in one breath and then, "I like the president candidate." He stuck a thumb into the air to show his support, before going quiet for the rest of the journey.

Ling's apartment on one of New York's most prized avenues was the sort of place that Zara had passed before, noticing how the shadows of imposing buildings echoed the structures' status by throwing themselves across the walkway and dominating across the street, too. Zara noticed how the beige granite rose into the cloudless Manhattan sky, golden eagles at each cornice. But for all its grandness on the outside, Ling's apartment on the inside was a warm, bright space with big couches, mismatched works of art and thick rugs into which Zara was welcomed. She was the last to arrive, and already a small group had gathered in Ling's kitchen.

The air was thick with the aroma of food that made Zara instantly hungry. Warm pastries, plates of out of season fruit, champagne, eggs and salmon were arranged across the counter top.

"Ling, I don't do salmon, where are the grits? Bacon? Eggs? Hash browns ..." said a man, his ageless face giving away nothing as he picked at something.

"I'm Chinese, Pedro. I don't do grits!"

"You're half Chinese, half American. And I want the American half to fix breakfast," the man continued.

"I don't cook. Well, I could try, but you wouldn't like it!" Ling added and handed Pedro a plate.

"I thought all good Chinese girls learn to cook?" Pedro asked, sweetly.

"I'm American," replied Ling smiling. "Now, meet Zara, my South African friend I was telling you about."

"You know, we were involved in the anti-apartheid movement when Luke and I were much younger and carefree, isn't that so Luke?" Pedro said, turning to look for Luke, who was on the other side of the room, engaged in what seemed to be a heated conversation with a woman who had been hastily introduced as Gianna. The woman nodded briefly at Zara, tossed back black hair that hit her shoulders at right angles, emphasising a bony structure, and continued speaking.

"But why they always have to say 'African-American' or 'black' before they say presidential candidate, but they not say of the other man 'white' – it's ridiculous ... " she was saying to Luke, her voice shrill as she slid rectangular black frames back up her nose. "I mean, why say every time?"

"Because, Gianna," Luke answered with deliberate patience. "This is a historic moment. We could have an African-American man become president. And so they mention his race because it is very relevant in the history of the US; they're making the point," Luke insisted.

"Oh and then of course, don't say he is both black and white because one group, they don't say it but we know they think he is not good enough to be called that, and the other group says he doesn't want to be called that anyway ... It's like a comedy, no?

And you all buy into it, madness ..." Gianna raised her hands to make the point.

"It's complex. And anyway, you're here and the whole world comes here at some point, and you always have so much to complain about," Luke replied, his face getting redder.

"Yes, yes, say nothing. Come, visit, bring your PhD and your labour, but don't comment on our wars or our politics, just eat our hamburgers and talk about how good our television is ...?" Gianna said, dismissing Luke as she turned towards the news programme that at that very moment showed the face of the presidential candidate in question.

"You two are being rude, this is not brunch as usual. Ling's invited someone," Pedro interrupted, walking Zara over to the other side of the room. "I was telling Zara how we were involved in the anti-apartheid movement when we were young ..."

"I don't ever remember being young," Luke said, smiling and pumping Zara's hand, his face smoothing to a healthy pink. "Sorry, Gianna knows how to get to me."

"Americans are so defensive ..." Gianna shot back.

"Come on now ..." Pedro said, but Ling was already taking Zara's arm and directing her to the other side of the room.

"Come and see my family from a safe distance," Ling said, as they walked to the wall where her family portraits hung. Some were modern renditions of her parents and herself and others were older, grainier pictures of family members, of generations gone by, dressed modestly, expressions stern.

"This is my family. And this, of course, is my father," she said, as Zara stood before a picture of an ageing man, white strands of hair threading his temples. The photograph had been positioned in the centre of the other portraits. "He is so disciplined, God! I don't know where he gets the energy or will, but he has it in buckets. He wakes up at five every morning, does tai chi, runs for a bit, then goes to the office and often works until midnight, sometimes seven days a week." She took a breath. "And this, of course, is my mom."

"Lovely family, your mom looks young," Zara decided as she touched the frame and stared into the face of a youthful-looking woman.

"Yeah well, Botox has its uses," Ling said, rolling her eyes. "What about your parents?"

"My mother passed away nearly a decade ago, from cancer. And my father died a few years back. So I suppose that makes me something of an orphan."

"Oh, I'm so sorry, I didn't know."

"Of course you didn't, that's alright," Zara said, gently.

When the morning was over, Zara was surprised at her sadness. She had seldom been in company recently, had chosen to isolate herself, a decision she now half regretted. She walked back to the station through Manhattan's Upper East Side. She wondered where everyone had to go, why people, even on Sunday, were hastily moving between places as if they had no choice but to keep going. Why hot chocolate was being consumed on sidewalks on a day that she remembered as being for big family lunches, followed by conversations and a snooze or leisurely drive.

But most of all she wondered about her father and the mismatch of it all. Things did not add up. They did not add up at all. The fury that had inhabited their household against government injustices did not quite fit with the missing years of her father's life and that inscrutable silence of his.

16

He *had* been a strange child, her father. You could see that even when he was an old man. The backward trajectory from a sexagenarian who was awkward in company, possibly even his own, who had preferred the company of dogs or books to people. Back, back the reel went until he was a strange little boy who liked to talk about war, who knew how long battles had lasted centuries before, who recreated massacres and retold stories better forgotten. Yes, that was Bart.

That Zara was born when her father was forty three didn't help. But then, he had loved to talk about history and to read, even aloud to his daughter. These were the things which softened Zara's recollections, she acknowledged begrudgingly.

*

A procession of women in house coats and head scarves left the employ of the Black family, apparently because of Bart. The women, it was said, would cover their ears, run from the child to find Hannah as she sat praying (a sudden new habit) or knitting long, colourfully un-wearable cardigans and the housekeepers would claim, "God, Antie, you should hear what say this child, I ask only what he's doing."

None of them stayed: Petunia, a sad brown-faced woman with brown hair and brown shoes who came from an invisible place called Up Country; Jezebel, a local girl from the Other Side of Town, who smelled of hunger and poorness and who cleaned and never spoke or made eye contact, and didn't return after the first week; and Ma Agnes, an old lady from the Other Other Side of Town with cracked black skin and hands fixed into spades that scooped things from the floor as she sang hymns in Xhosa, first softly, and then so loudly (to cover the child's talking) that Hannah claimed Ma Agnes was disturbing her prayer time and asked her to leave.

Even Hannah, who had once understood him so well, began signing the cross or knitting maniacally when Bart spoke of some war fact he had learned.

"Good lordy child! Millions dead you say … may God forgive," she'd say, tugging hard at the ball of wool wrapped around her ankles.

By then Hannah had turned to God for everything. Months after that summer reading when a stranger's beauty changed their lives, Hannah had moved a single bed into the room that her eldest daughter Martha had vacated when she married the local shopkeeper's son. Martha's room left empty, Hannah erected a shrine to Jesus and Mary and a determination to make God the most important man in her life.

Eventually Bart did learn to keep his untidy thoughts where they could not be seen. So Bart grew alone and the history inside of him found no exit, until many, many years later.

*

The film must be wound to 1948 because that was where the real story of Bart began; when he turned eighteen and was accepted into the local University's law school.

Coloured and Native boys fill last two places in University's law department.

The daily paper reported in a rectangle of news; a cutting that deserved a full page in Hannah's crowded photo album.

Zara did not mind this bit of vanity from her grandmother because it was a big year, perhaps the most important for decades to come. 1948, Zara had never needed a book to tell her, was the year apartheid was legislated. The English and Afrikaner Union government had been defeated by The National Party, under D.F. Malan. That year, the widely adhered segregation practices devised early in the century had become law, and government would restrict yet more freedoms, outlawing marriages between people of different colours. Soon individuals would be classified, and different races allocated to separate homes, neighbourhoods, schools and churches. Land was to be confiscated and populations relocated, the sharing of cinema and bus seats made illegal, and the pass (the documents introduced when Zara's grandfather Isaiah was a boy, stopping the free movement of black people) would be more stringently implemented.

*

There they sat: Bart and James Ndlovu, in a huge white room beneath a fan spinning overhead. At least this was how Zara conjured up that lovely university on the foot of a mountain as it looked decades before, its huge old rooms, passages, and ivy-clad stone walls.

Surely Bart's gaze drifted from the droning of his lecturer down, down to Marybeth Harrison's legs as they swung from a yellow or possibly blue sundress that made her skin seem papery and lucent.

They were an extraordinary trio: Bart, James and Marybeth – she a petite thing, and one of four women in that year's class. Each of the three represented the university's nod to change, perhaps one day far in the future, but right then, the act of friendship itself was also one of resistance. This combination of people in an equal relationship: banned. Even if they glossed over this law denouncing association, what could they do? Being seen in public would bring confrontation or worse, arrest. So they clung to the sidelines, hanging in Marybeth's flat listening to jazz, studying together, meeting in the shadows of libraries. Bart had often spoken of James Ndlovu, after all, his story was fable: how this son of a headman had been educated in a missionary school, and had travelled from Zululand on a train bound for Cape Town in the year that apartheid became law. Eventually, he graduated amongst the top of the class.

After the room had filtered out that day, Marybeth Harrison walked over to where the two men sat and rested a hip gingerly against their desk.

"How are things in your ivory tower?" she asked, motioning to the untouched desks surrounding Bart and James, like a bomb clearing.

"I think the valley is where the real power rests in this room," James answered, completing his notes, but smiling beneath his eyebrows. His face, already then had the bearing of greatness – cheek bones that shone beneath his skin, eyes that never reflected sentiment, lips that smiled only when he commanded them to do so.

"Quite," Marybeth replied. "Well, I wondered, seeing as you two seem so lonely, whether you would like to come to a little gathering I am having this weekend. Small thing, a few friends."

"Yes, of course, we will be there Marybeth," James answered quickly, and on behalf of Bart, because it was plain to see he was the decision maker.

*

In the early days the meetings were held in Marybeth's flat, on the top floor of a small block. How had they become involved? Bart's answer to this question from his curious daughter who wanted to know everything: *We fell into it how could we not after all what else was there it was our duty politics was in the air we were forced by circumstances we answered a call there was liberation or nothing else.*

Yes, Father, Zara thought mordantly to herself so many years later.

They would have gathered Saturday after Saturday in Marybeth's flat discussing, analysing, reading aloud from books. Which ones? Zara went in close: Lenin or Marx? Wasn't that the order of the day? A print by Toulouse Lautrec hanging overhead. The mountain barely in the distance, framed by the window. Groups like those made up of teachers, workers or students gathered in rooms similar and dissimilar across town so that they could discuss the finer details of the laws falling in place and dividing cities into quarrelsome zones. Sulkily appreciative of the deftness, the cunning of their enemy, because that was what they agreed they had: an enemy.

But, it was what was happening beneath the table that Zara was interested in: two hands folded around each other. Two legs intertwined. Bart and Marybeth and the awakening of a truly illicit love.

To Zara it felt like a betrayal. Her mother's husband: Bart with another woman, even if it were decades before the fact. Still, Zara looked earnestly in on them for the sake of fact finding. Her mind closed to the sting of their union.

*

It began with liaisons in the library where Marybeth occasionally glanced up from her books to find Bart staring at her, and slowly progressed to Sunday afternoon tea. Soon Bart could not tell his own taste in music from his lover's, could not decide whether he had picked the red tie that he wore whenever he wanted to please Marybeth (which was often) and didn't know any longer where he began from where Marybeth did.

Their romance had to be held in secret. Marybeth continued to occupy her place in the first row of the lecture hall, only speaking to Bart about private matters when they were alone. Unlike other campus lovers who draped themselves across each other, Bart and Marybeth's relationship was made more interesting by the fact that it was, after all, illicit.

They ate their lunch and drank their coffee at separate tables at the campus canteen, each ordering the identical meal in the hope that they would taste the same food. No longer seated together in the library, they sat at separate tables but read the same book so that they knew, even apart, that they shared the same thoughts. When they walked to her flat, they did so on opposite sides of the pavement, the one's stride trying to match the other's as they giggled privately. When they arrived, Marybeth always entered her flat first, followed by Bart minutes later. At times, when they were feeling especially young and carefree, they met up with James and his girlfriend, and together the couples sat in the semi-light of jazz clubs which purposefully ignored the country's laws, or ate in crowded restaurants which were known for their lack of attention to all government regulations.

Their love affair would last until Marybeth was ushered out of the country, away one night to a safe home in a cold country on the other side of the world.

17

Above, the sky was impossible to read as an insouciant sun came out, changed its mind, came out and changed its mind again. Still, below, spring had been decided upon and on Bloomfield Avenue, blossoms were bursting from trees, grass was wheedling through the newly defrosted earth so that sharp green needles were just visible. It had all resulted in a human chain reaction: stalls were brought forth to sell organic produce, crocheted bags, brass earrings and mismatched cups, and all manner of people had taken up residence on the sidewalk. It was also Zara's birthday.

Leaning out of the window, Zara took in the commotion.

"My friend, the day is wonderful," Mr Ortez from the tobacco store called hopefully from below as he spotted Zara overhead.

"I see that ..." Zara replied, showing him her crossed fingers, before she turned back into her room and prepared for the call which she, Amy and Aunty Rose had scheduled via Skype to mark the day.

Today the cousins would communicate with each other as real, whole people, not the discombobulated voices that came drifting up phone lines – but fleshly people with arms, legs, pimples and all; ah, the marvels of modern technology that wouldn't even register with Zara and Amy, accustomed as they were to it, while Rose would shake her head and acknowledge that the world was beyond her.

"Zee, happy happy birthday!" Amy said, as Zara came into focus. Aunty Rose, dressed smartly, was seated beside her daughter, smiling a camera-ready smile. "What will you do today?" Amy asked.

"I don't know yet. But I have a hankering for milk tart," said Zara, sending Aunty Rose running for her recipe book.

"Four cups of milk – four, a stick of cinnamon, vanilla pod, butter – lots of it," she went on, and Zara did not have the heart to tell her that she had nowhere to bake.

"And you, how are *you*?" Zara asked eventually, the milk tart recipe scribbled onto a page for Aunty Rose's sake.

"Good, good," Amy said, nonchalantly.

"Good? Where? The ruling party is imploding – that's how that professor on the television said it, imploding! And tell her what happened to you Amy, go ahead, tell her!" Aunty Rose countered.

"Mummy, don't start ... there was a strike recently, that's all," Amy said, smiling and winking at Zara, a sign that it was about to begin.

"A strike, that's all? The *nurses* were striking! Tried to stop Amy from going to work ..."

"Their pay is low, conditions are poor, they had a strike, it was resolved," Amy said defensively, giving Zara the impression that she was now viewed as being on the other side: the world of opinion far from home.

Perhaps this was so. Zara had seen tales of home magnified and horrified through the prism of a television screen; read a million miles away by an anchor with obscenely white teeth and who, try as he may, couldn't quite hide his disapproval. Never mind life between news clips. Happiness, boredom and all that. No, Africa, all of it – *the whole country* (a prominent American politician had said) – was permanently miserable. Even Zara seemed to take notice of what a warring, starving, disease infested, utterly forsaken place home was.

"They stopped you from working, Amy?" Zara probed gently.

"Of course not, these are my colleagues, friends. They didn't harass me, just asked me not to work. I disagreed and that was that."

"Huh! She had to go around the back like a blinking criminal. This country ..." Aunty Rose said, pulling her face into a line of distaste.

"Anyway," Zara interrupted, changing subject at Amy's resigned silence. "Aunty Rose, I wanted to ask you. There was a friend my father knew at university. Do you remember the name Marybeth Harrison?"

"Who?"

"Marybeth. They were friends ... my father spoke about her ... after my mom ..." Zara said, and quietly erased the word *died*. No one used this word in relation to Lena. The word, the concept itself, somehow belittled her – so full of life, even in death, her memory burning through the decades.

"Marybeth ... Marybeth ... yes," Rose said, stumbling into the past. A world she had considerably more patience for than the present. "My goodness ... they were an item for years. We thought it might lead to marriage ... I mean this was before your mother ... but it was banned then you know."

"Why are you asking about an old fling of your dad's, Zara?" Amy interjected.

"I thought perhaps she might have been involved in what happened with my dad."

"Oh, I wouldn't know if she is still alive even. She left in the 60's ... exile ... I think. Long ago. She was a wildcard. Full of ideas, very involved in politics. Never knew what she would say next," Aunty Rose added.

"But you don't know which country she moved to?"

"Oh heavens no. We weren't close like that. I just knew her because she was friends with your father ... no ..."

"Do you know why she left? Did they end their relationship before then?" Zara persisted.

"No my girl, you are asking the wrong person. But probably she eventually got into trouble because of something she said or wrote. Sometimes she was in the papers ... she was a communist!" cried Aunty Rose.

"Zee – are you sure this is the right way to approach things?" Amy interrupted, and for the first time Zara noticed how tired she looked. "I mean, why not demand that the government provide you with facts? Instead of this wandering into history. What's the point of all of this ... this research? And, if you push them they have to relent. Write enough letters, make enough noise, and eventually you get what you want, trust me I know," Amy said, defining her method for dealing with incompetence or problems of any sort. "Persevere."

"They won't give you the time of day," shot out Aunty Rose.

"Zee," Amy went on agitatedly, "there are many challenges, but they can only get resolved when people tackle them head on." Zara began to understand that there was another conversation going on.

"Amy, I didn't say I wouldn't come back," Zara said quietly.

"Don't! Don't!" Aunty Rose called out from a face tight as cling wrap.

"Just don't get thrown off course, alright?" Amy added; Zara knew the conversation was ending.

Amy and Aunty Rose wished Zara a happy birthday again, and then they were gone to squabble on their own time.

*

When Zara arrived at campus, Ling was already there, a cup of coffee and a cupcake waiting on her desk.

"What's this?" Zara asked, surprised.

"Happy birthday!"

"How did you know?"

"There is a calendar for birthdays up in reception. Not that anyone else notices."

"Thank you. This looks decadent," Zara said, scraping off a bit of chocolate icing and plopping it into her mouth.

"Oh I have more," Ling added, pointing to a jovial pink, purple and white striped box.

"I didn't think anyone knew. Thank you Ling, really."

"Hey, we have to look after each other, you and me ... being outsiders, and all."

"Are we ... outsiders ... I mean?" Zara asked, taking a bite.

"Yes ... no ... there will always be somewhere else that calls me, even if I end up with the American dream, husband, kids ... there will always be this other place that I belong. On the other hand, where else would my family have gone, and where else would my father have made *his* dreams come true?" she said, seriously.

"And you? Could it ever become home for you?"

"I'm not sure," Zara answered, and as she began to gravitate to her desk, Ling stood abruptly, "No, don't sit. We're taking off. New Jersey must have a park somewhere in all this dullness ... let's go find it."

For the first time in months, Zara agreed to forget Cape Town, Timbuktu, even history itself.

18

The past demanded its share of the present, and Zara wearily made her way back to her desk at night, determined to cut into the heart of it. There were questions for which she was determined to find answers: what had her father's alleged crime been? When and why had he stopped practising law, and had Marybeth Harrison's departure anything to do with her father?

Zara wrote to James Ndlovu, Bart's one-time friend, today a high court judge. She phrased her questions carefully – in case he did not already know about the accusations against Bart – instead asking about her father's time as a lawyer and his political involvement.

Zara had last seen Judge Ndlovu at her father's funeral. The meeting had been strained – before that they had not seen each other since she was a teenager, and with the slow chaos of a funeral, the time had not been right for a reunion.

Still, James Ndlovu had made the trip to Cape Town for the burial, so Zara knew the bonds of their friendship still held.

*

By the age of thirty Bart had moved into his own house in the District, a little area five minutes by foot from that magnificent family home on the hill flourishing beneath its army of trees.

During their Sunday afternoon drives, Zara and her parents often passed by the semi-detached house into which Bart had once lived.

A mountain as a backdrop, the houses sloped downward into adjoining white cottages like a neat row of teeth. She remembered the humming of their laughter after they passed the houses on one such drive, aghast that someone had painted one of the cottages beige.

"Only in this city ..." Lena had said implacably, "... a gap in the mouth ... just like the Cape Town smile ..." referencing the unforgiveable seventies fad of front-teeth-extractions which had set Lena in battle against her students for following, in her words, the most deplorable fashion trend ever begun.

During the many afternoon drives when they passed the house in which Bart had once lived, Zara wanted to climb out of the car, in order to touch the walls of the house, examine them and place them. The house was a narrow little space with a lounge that hung off the back, a tiny bedroom, bathroom and a kitchen just big enough; Bart had said this much.

On those lazy Sunday afternoons, as Zara stuck her head out of the car's window to see what she could see, she might have peered down the passageway of one such house, to the small courtyard at the other end, and, if she pushed her body further still, her waist balancing on the car door, conversations could be drifted into, because no one's talk was private on that road.

Bart would linger for only a moment longer, his foot gently on the accelerator of their *Volksie* (an orange VW Beetle) before pulling suddenly away: uphill – a slow escape on roads that tilted madly towards the moon. After that, the afternoon trailed off into silence.

*

For the history of the District there was plenty: books, novels, documentaries, plays, even musicals. So Zara knew the stories about the politics, intellectuals, gangsters, tales of revolutionaries and drunks living, working and debating side by side – a community that Zara could barely conjure: diverse in religion and race. She often believed, though, that the stories must have arisen out of the sadness that followed when the area was levelled and the residents of the District moved elsewhere, anywhere, as part of the government's Slum Clearing Act. Stories grown from heartache. No matter; despite the eternal shrine erected in the minds of those who had lived there, she never could find someone to deny that this was how it really was, after all.

Regardless of what she knew from legend, Zara had days earlier visited the Berwick Library. Searching for what, she did not know, until she had in her hands a pamphlet, so old that the stiffened leaves had whispered as she turned them. In it, a piece that had made her hands tremble: her father's girlfriend from university, Marybeth Harrison's name beneath an article: *White Resistance: voices against Apartheid.*

Impatiently Zara had traced each word with her finger. The book was treasonous in its time, and Zara wondered at the events that must have transpired in that little house.

*

The family next door was having soup for dinner again. They never had enough, but even so, they always sent over food for Bart. This was a detail Zara recalled from her father's rare stories of his life then. What had he said?

"There was a sense of community ... not like nowadays ... no one talks to their neighbours now ... but then we knew everyone on the street ... and my neighbours ... the Meyer's ... no, no the ... shit, I can't remember their name ... *Duimpie*, they called the father ... short, oblong man, like a thumb ... they sent over food every night for a year to thank me for helping their son once ... a good family ... you children will never know what they bull-dozed ... what was lost."

There was also the wind.

Zara imagined that a Cape Town winter had blown in on the back of one of those winds that, if caught at the right moment, sounded like howling children left to fend for themselves.

Of course, the walls of Bart's house were cool to the touch and clammy when it rained, causing him to tug at the blanket around his shoulders, warm his hands with his breath, as he tried to focus on the work before him.

"Have you read the day's paper?" It was Marybeth, sashaying in as she did, in a dark maroon dress. Her lips were too red, her eyelids too blue, despite her bravery and the cold, despite the fact that she was a lawyer who had come from a gruelling day of work. But how else could Zara see this woman who was warming space for her mother?

"What does it say?" Bart asked as he continued to read from a stack of books.

"The Bantu Education Act is going through. Children, *African* children will be taught their place in this world: taught to become labourers, an underclass," she answered, heaviness in her voice, her hands trembling as they always did.

Bart shook his head. "What can be done?"

"The same: meet, march, protest," Marybeth said wearily, because protests sprang up as fervently and as quickly as the new laws.

"What else is there?" Bart turned and looked at Marybeth.

"Something more," she said, and raised a finger to her lips. The house next door had gone silent.

"They have gone to bed," Bart said.

"You trust everyone," she snapped, and waited to be certain that the residents next door had wandered deep into their house, where at least their love-making and dreams were sacred. "They don't like me, you know. Is it too much to send over two plates?" she said, walking over to her handbag, extracting a long thin cigarette and lighting it.

"Marybeth, you know they can't afford to even send over one. And I told them not to, but they insist because I helped the boy with his homework. He is bright ... anyway, my family likes you," Bart smiled.

He was handsome then, a head of curly black hair, his face open and unlined, far before it was set with worry and disappointments.

"And you said your sisters would like any girl with blue eyes," she said, puffing viciously.

"I said that? No, I was mistaken, they only like certain girls with blue eyes," Bart said, trying to soften the line of conversation.

"The old lady doesn't greet me. She watches me as if I am the trouble." A cord of ash disjointed itself, and hit the floor with an imperceptible *ploof.*

"People are afraid. If someone reports us, they could get into trouble too. And everyone could be evicted at any time, moved out to the townships. And they have heard your politics."

"Yes, they have heard through the walls," Marybeth said, and tapped quietly against the thin divide, stubbing out the cigarette with her free hand in a glass dish that swivelled wildly.

"Your name has become synonymous with leaders who have been imprisoned. They know how involved you are, maybe they don't know why."

She walked over to her handbag, took out a second cigarette, then changed her mind. "I am going to bed," Marybeth said, from the doorway where she had stopped momentarily before vanishing into the house.

19

It was the end of the week. Ling had bought tickets to see a play that had been all the rage in Europe that summer, showing at a local theatre, the Radomsky in Claremont, New Jersey.

In fact, a bus load of jaded New Yorkers arrived too. While some Manhattan residents were hungry for a bite of life away from the Big Apple, inhabitants of the idyllic town of Claremont, New Jersey, drove in the opposite direction towards Broadway to escape the boredom of the suburbs.

The Radomsky Theatre commandeered the finery of the small town of Claremont like a thumb in a pie.

The theatre's metallic beams jutted in random directions and left traces of multi-coloured light in the clear evening sky, while its glass walls held the neighbouring woods in a synthetic glow. The glass floor, suspended between robotic-like legs that reached deep into the earth, hovered meters above the ground, so that bits of unexcavated rock and a dry river bed were vertiginously visible from the theatre's bar. Zara read from a torn magazine page stuck with a tack to the notice board that the theatre was a structural marvel with its '... sleek lines, cool interiors and minimalist aesthetic'. It was the result of an over-generous endowment from the eponymous billionaire who had spent his early years playing in those woods, climbing those trees. Zara wondered why then he had fled to the anonymity and energy of the metropolis next door.

Standing beside Gianna, the angular woman she had met before, Zara indulged in small talk, commenting on the spectacle of nature outside the theatre, while Ling and her friends, Luke and Pedro, sipped drinks at the bar.

"Something is very frightening about these trees," Gianna suggested to Zara, "I don't like it ..." she added softly.

But before Zara could answer, the conversation that Luke and Pedro had been quietly whittling away at, spilled into public domain.

"The waiter did not ignore you!" Luke said, an irate note entering his voice.

"Yeah, he did. He absolutely did," Pedro answered.

"He would have got to you, but he went to check on whether I could get a Mojito which is not on the menu. He was gonna come back, he probably just got side-tracked." Luke looked behind him, to his right, to the second floor, as if this might conjure the waiter.

"So, I'm paranoid?" Zara heard the challenge in Pedro's voice.

"Of course you are, you're a New Yorker. And every time we go outside of Manhattan you say people are either ignoring us because you're black and I'm not, or because we're gay," Luke said, completely oblivious to the small crowd who gently turned their ears in the direction of the conversation or angled their heads in an effort to fine-tune.

"Does that make me wrong? Or them?"

"Let's just focus on something else," said Luke, suddenly staring at Zara as he realised that they had been overheard.

Zara couldn't help but wonder what her father and Marybeth of the 1950s might have thought about *this* conversation and *this* presidential election, and how matters so staunchly defended by so many in one era could be thought of as madness only a generation later.

"Because we have a black man running for president, I'm suddenly not allowed to say that someone or something is 'racist'. Or 'prejudiced'. Or 'discriminatory'. And when he doesn't win?" Pedro asked, taking a slurp from his drink.

"It's time to transcend ... we should be talking post race ... and he might win," Luke tried to say pleasantly, though to Zara's ears it came out flat.

"Well tell you what, I'll talk 'post race,'" Pedro replied, "when people no longer lock their car doors as I walk by ... post race!" Pedro muttered and turned to Zara. "What do you think?"

"I'm starting to feel more at home," Zara replied. "I read the other day that most South Africans agree that race still informs everything, and only a handful feel differently. And they, well, they are mostly young, with some advantages ..." Zara replied, noting that she had been consulted, though she hardly felt an expert.

"And then sometimes, often even, you find people who always need a cause ... who are addicted to the suffering ..." interjected Luke.

"Yes, don't forget I spend my life with you ..." Pedro answered before the final bell chimed, signalling the beginning of the play. The conversation was left hanging and the audience of onlookers turned away disappointed.

Zara sat in the first balcony of the Radomsky Theatre. The pair of heels that she had felt bold enough to buy a few days back, in a moment that she had begun to think of as pure folly, was loose and dangling around her ankles.

She had lost concentration on the scene before her. The actress – silent, naked and draped in transparent white had been drifting around the stage to the backdrop of Mozart's *The Magic Flute* for some ten minutes. Before that the Italian Theatre Company had sat lined up on chairs, much like the one Zara was seated in, staring from the stage at a bemused audience. The programme notes indicated that this was a commentary on contemporary war-time apathy. After all, this was a country at war on two fronts.

But what truly dawned on Zara as she sat in the half-light of the Radomsky Theatre was that she was starting to feel alright. That perhaps she was even beginning to think that the past might at some point be left behind. It wasn't a momentous feeling, but all the same, there it was.

20

The email from James Ndlovu one week later brought with it a thunderstorm, undoing whatever calm had begun tentatively to settle on Zara's life.

The judge would be in New York for a week and had enquired whether Zara could make it to his hotel at 3p.m. that Sunday.

It was not so much an invitation as a request for her to be in attendance, Zara decided as she stepped off the train from New Jersey. After all, he was a high court judge back home and, despite the fact that she had got to know him from afar through stories that her father had told her and occasional news reports, she understood that he was not the sort one turned down.

*

The hotel on New York's Upper West Side was famed for its views of Central Park, its eponymously named salad, and its celebrities. As Zara walked to the front desk she felt her shabbiness, from the half-moons beneath her eyes due to long hours spent writing at night, to the jeans which fell around her hips from a hopelessly inadequate diet of apples and coffee.

She passed beneath a grotesquely huge chandelier clinking seconds from her head, stared back as eight foot mirrors reflected her in series, and walked on towards the front desk where an enormous armchair had swallowed a little boy, leaving only his feet dangling helplessly.

Zara took the lift to the judge's room, arriving precisely at 3p.m. The judge was seated on the sofa of his suite reading the paper, the door slightly ajar. Zara rapped quickly on the door before walking in.

"Ah, you're a sight for sore eyes," he said, rising to greet her.

"And you, Judge Ndlovu. It's been much too long."

"What is this language of strangers? Judge? It's Uncle James! Much too long indeed! Come and give me a hug," he said, and folded her into his black suit as Zara reciprocated awkwardly.

"Now let me see how you've grown. Yes. Zara. You know I named you, don't you? I had come down to Cape Town and was visiting with your father when he said to me, 'James if it's a girl, what should I call her?' And of course a princess should be called such, hence Zara. Or do you know that story? No, have you heard it before?" He asked throwing his arms open and laughing fully because he always told her this, while her mother had an entirely different telling for how her name had been decided. Zara smiled politely, discomfited by this great man's language and the delineation of power, so quickly established.

"Come sit," he said, beckoning to the sofa across from his.

Zara sat on the golden floral couch and assessed her father's old friend. He wore a well-fitting suit, pressed perfectly, his finger nails glinting in the strands of light that had found its way into the room on the nineteenth floor.

Over tea they spoke about home, the other's wellbeing and

exchanged news, before the judge looked carefully at Zara and finally came to the reason for their meeting.

"I received an email from you some weeks ago, Zara," he said slowly, stretching his fingers into a bridge before placing them delicately on his lap. "I'm sorry I didn't respond immediately, but I didn't quite know how to answer your questions. I travel to New York every second month ... I am part of a commission here ... so I thought to let it wait until I could speak to you face to face."

"Sounds serious."

"No, no ..." he began, but stopped short. "Your questions ... they surprised me."

"I just ... I suppose I was just interested to find out more about my father's past. What his involvement had been ... with you ... the struggle ..." Zara proceeded slowly.

"Yes, your father. As you know Zara, he was a dear friend of mine. I felt almost blessed to meet him. I had travelled by train, you know, took a train and two buses from my village in Natal ..." his eyes found a corner of the ceiling, "... my first journey anywhere ... but I was a headman's son, and my father was what one might call progressive for a man of his era ... no son of his would be without a Western education. He sent me to a mission school ... then on to Cape Town to study law or medicine. I hated the sight of blood, still do," the judge's face pained at the thought.

"Yes, I have heard," Zara said, shifting restlessly. She knew this story too.

"The trains were divided: *Net Blankes* up in the front with the good seats. So I had to walk past the first carriages until I reached the place for blacks. The indignity of it was incredible ... we journeyed to Cape Town without a toilet on our side of the train ... we had to wait until the train stopped along the way ... of course not everyone could ..."

"Yes, Judge," Zara said respectfully, before she took the pause to interrupt him. "But I need to ask you about my father, what his involvement in politics was, in the movement. Your own participation is well documented."

The judge looked at her sharply, or was it hurt that she saw?

"Your father? Well, yes, in a way everyone was, but it wasn't really your father's thing. Bart was more a man of law, he was fascinated by the way the thing worked ... apartheid as an ideology, a construct ... and he preferred defending people to attending meetings, planning, being at the coalface, so to speak. In the beginning we had many meetings, reading groups they were called, at a friend's flat in Rondebosch. He attended those, but then, maybe he had his reasons. Nonetheless, he probably did his share ... but, why is it that you ask?" The judge looked pointedly at Zara.

"I received a letter from the government some months back ... it seems to implicate him in some sort of betrayal against the movement," she began slowly.

"I had heard that letters were being sent out ... that there was a sort of reckoning taking place ... keeping noisemakers in their place ... members of the judiciary not excluded," he replied, swiping at invisible bits of fluff on his knees.

"What do you think?" Zara asked with more boldness than she felt.

"I think ... I don't know what to think," the judge said, smiling briefly, as he shifted to the edge of the sofa. He had the movements of a much younger man, Zara noticed, yet he would have been the same age as her father. "What did that letter say?"

"I have it with me." Zara reached into her bag and handed him the fold of paper.

James Ndlovu sat quietly and read the letter, then reread it more thoroughly before he brushed his crop of white hair with his hand, stood up and went to survey Central Park from his window.

"What a long day this has been," he said quietly, before he turned and addressed her. "I don't know what to say."

"Tell me what you know. Could he have been a traitor? An informer perhaps?"

"Zara that is a question I don't think any child should have to ask. But because you have asked I will tell you what I can."

"Yes." She moved to the edge of her seat too.

"When we finished studying I left for Johannesburg. While your father and a friend of ours, Marybeth ..."

"... Harrison, yes, I know about your friendship."

"Do you?" the judge's tone was brisk.

"She and my father were together, weren't they?"

"Yes, yes of course they were. They remained in Cape Town when I left. They both did their articles at local attorneys' offices. Progressive companies. What I know is that Marybeth became very involved once I left. She joined the movement. Became a vocal advocate for the struggle. As did I. Bart ... well, like I said. He preferred the finer details of defence law. He didn't attend the meetings, but he was, shall we say, a supporter of the cause."

"But he *was* supportive?" She could hear the undercurrent of pleading in her own voice.

"Sometimes, often, he worked for free, giving legal counsel ... many, if not most, could not pay ..."

"Could there have been a chance that he might have informed ... or perhaps someone else blamed him for something which they had done, or overheard perhaps?"

"I wouldn't have thought it when I knew him ..." he faced her fully, "... but towards the end of their relationship, Marybeth visited me sometimes in Johannesburg and we wondered about some things which we knew had reached the security police. Things only a few people knew ... someone who knew us was speaking."

"And you think he may have informed on his girlfriend and closest friend?" Zara stood too.

"No, no ... I'm not ... I don't know ... but there were things which they knew ..."

"But why would he do such a thing?" Zara asked, closing the gap between them until she was close enough to smell his spicy cologne.

The judge looked away from her and announced suddenly, "Look, this wasn't a good idea to speak so hurriedly. There is a lot to explain. But I have to go to a meeting in twenty minutes, Zara, perhaps you can come back tomorrow? I know it will be Monday, but if you could, maybe we could speak some more then?"

"Yes, of course, you said you could only meet for a short while, I remember that you said that. I will go into work late, I could do that. I will see you tomorrow morning then. Would nine suit you?"

"I will buy you breakfast," the judge replied, not quite relaxing as he accompanied Zara to the door.

Zara called Ling and asked if she could spend the night and Ling was delighted. There was no sense in going all the way home.

Zara walked the more than fifteen blocks without stopping.

She was troubled by their conversation and the realisation that the judge knew something. His face had carried an accusation, or resentment, or was it guilt?

Evening was falling as Zara arrived at Ling's apartment.

"I am meeting a friend, in fact I was planning to introduce you two," Ling said, as Zara entered and realised it was too late to back slowly out of the door.

"Actually, I'm a little tired Ling, I thought we could get some dinner and then I was hoping to crash here for the evening."

"That's what I had in mind," Ling said smiling, so that Zara knew she was trapped.

Dinner was not a simple affair. Ling had invited a suspiciously single friend to meet them at an Italian restaurant.

"This is Michael ... he's a freelance writer."

"Ling, he better be here for you ... " Zara grabbed her friend's arm urgently after Michael had excused himself briefly.

"What? What do you think of me?" Ling replied, flickering her eyes dramatically. "Listen, it's just dinner. But he's cute and nice and you probably need to hang with a man occasionally ..."

"Oh God, I've had such a rough day ... don't you dare disappear."

"Fine. But just so you know there is a Chinese saying: a little romance is good for the soul."

"That is *not* a Chinese saying!"

"Isn't it?" said Ling, smiling fully into her drink.

21

Zara awoke to the sound of sirens on a summer morning.

Her mind cleared as sleep departed.

Much of the talk the previous evening had been frivolous: what Michael, a native Californian down to his sun-kissed skin, loved about New York: a walking city, every kind of person from here to Timbuktu (Zara had smiled at his metaphor), the pizza, the snow (no scrap that), the music, the Arts. And what he hated: impoliteness, police sirens, traffic, subway rats.

Zara had liked him sufficiently but skirted around any sort of follow up meeting. After all, she was not interested in a romance.

Her last serious relationship had ended months before she'd left South Africa. Antonio had packed a duffel bag and announced that he would be travelling around India until he knew what he wanted from life, before suggesting half-heartedly that Zara go with him. She'd chosen home and career instead. He had been one more person in a line of relationships that had not worked. Thami had proposed marriage. "But it's only been seven months," Zara had blurted, stunned. And before that had been Ian, *the one.* Zara had been reduced to clichés around him, she remembered regretfully.

For some of her generation – the sort that hung around universities and theatres – maturing in a post-apartheid country, race, class and religion were no longer limiting factors in romance or friendship. Her boyfriends and friends had reflected this, and Zara had assumed naively that for everyone else too love was all that mattered. But then Ian had introduced Zara to his family whom he promised couldn't care less about race or pedigree (though they, apparently, were descended from a royal line, said Ian's mother, before adding that of course that sort of thing didn't matter now-a-days). No, Zara had agreed.

Ian, the self-deprecating economics lecturer hadn't thought that it mattered either: "Who cares what your grandfather did or didn't do ... although probably we shouldn't mention family trees and that sort of thing ... we'll say you don't know your history ... besides they'll find such talk irrelevant ..."

They had not. As all five members of Ian's clan had floated their silver spoons above broth served by employees who stared suspiciously at Zara (perhaps wondering how she had landed on that side of the table) they'd spoken of how they had never ever supported the old South African government, deplored apartheid absolutely, had always loved Mandela and Tutu and oh, as an after-thought, would she mind terribly if they enquired about her family tree?

For weeks she had carried a grudge, while Ian seemed to fall into a new sort of discomfort that eventually became an almighty wall between them, until the romance slowly, agonizingly, had run out of fuel.

Zara walked to the window with a cup of coffee she had made from a sachet of instant grains, which she had found in Ling's otherwise forsaken kitchen. Ling had already left for campus.

It would be a magnificent day, Zara decided, holding her breath at the apartment's sky-scraping eye on Manhattan. The sun was already slicing away from golden carapaces of domes and pyramids that stood atop long, elegant constructions. Perhaps she would get lost here, after all, Zara decided. Fall into another world that was clean and clear of history.

Every time she spoke with Amy or Aunty Rose, something else seemed to come undone at home.

"The television news says that the president is going to get kicked out by the other fellow. Kicked out! And, more protests ... service delivery this time," Aunty Rose had complained the last time Zara had called home.

"Well what do you expect? Half of the country and almost all of my patients don't even have a proper roof above their heads, Mummy. The government has fallen asleep," Amy had retorted in the background, a little too ferociously.

"I thought you loved this government."

"I. Love. The. Country! I'm loyal to people, not people in power," she'd shouted back.

Amy was unflinching. Zara had always known this to be the detail that set Amy apart from everyone else. Amy didn't retreat when spirit was needed. If hospital management needed to be confronted, it was she who was sent ahead to do the work. And with Rose, Amy soldiered on, never abandoning her post, despite the fact that her mother seemed the bane of her existence: virtually opposite from her daughter in every way that counted and even in the way they looked. Where Amy was curvaceous and red headed with large brown freckles covering her delicate skin, her mother was petite and dark and sharp.

If there were a universal score card somewhere matching intention to action, Amy might very well approach a perfect mark. As for Zara, well, she doubted she would make the list at all, she decided, as she watched a bird take flight from the top of a building.

*

Zara arrived at the hotel a little after nine. She had misjudged the walking distance and had arrived ten minutes later than expected. She knocked on the door of the judge's suite, dismayed when minutes later she was still standing there. Zara went back down to the front desk.

"Judge N-da-lo-voo?" the receptionist managed with difficulty, mangling his name. "No, I'm sorry, he's checked out already."

"But I had an appointment with him for nine this morning," Zara replied, stunned. He was a man of his word, surely.

"Well, he has left, and anyway," the receptionist added acidly, "it is past a quarter after."

"Could you check if he left me a note?" Zara asked.

The receptionist scratched about in the cubby holes behind her. "What did you say your name was?"

"Zara Black."

"Oh yeah, he left something, here you go."

Dear Zara

I am sorry to have left without following up our conversation. But something urgent has come up in Johannesburg and I had to take an earlier flight home.

But I am in New York regularly. Perhaps we can meet again.

Love, Uncle James

22

It was in a fit of dread that she could not quite explain to herself that Zara took the train back to New Jersey, and returned directly to her room on Bloomfield Avenue.

There were things that she wanted to capture which only now had started to make sense. It had begun to dawn on her that her father's secrets were there, in the centre of their lives all the while and if she only prised open her memory, she would find them. What her mother must have known! All Zara had to do was reach across the wretchedness of her mother's death, and travel back to their house on that long dry road.

*

There was a scene: her mother seated in the lounge in perpetual grey and solitude. Why was she so sullen?

But then Lena hated their little home and needed no other reason to be unhappy. She had often spoken about the day when they had moved into their house: Zara had been barely a month old. Lena had stood on the *stoep*, noticing with dismay how their house faced the same tar road that strung together thirty other houses with the exact specifications as their own. Not that it mattered. Because there was no ocean, no harbour, no mountain; only a single tree that the Cape City Council had planted in the middle of the garden – to provoke sympathy and curiosity like a stranger at a party, Lena had said.

She had always been quick off the mark. Caustic, Bart had called it. A dark humour that cut through fools.

"Are you ready to leave?" Bart walked into the lounge. His temples were silver, and he carried a frown across his brows.

"I already told you I am not going," she replied, as Zara sat in the corner flipping through a magazine.

"But we agreed yesterday. He has asked to see us. It's been a long time and I think I should go," Bart said, standing beneath a watercolour that Lena had painted in one of her blue moods: *The Trinidad*, a lone boat, tossed far out on a restive sea.

"Just yesterday we were not allowed there for anything but to clean or beg and today we take tea like the royal family and their dogs? But who will play the corgis in this production?" Lena objected to the invitation at the city's most expensive hotel. "Anyway," she concluded, "how *can* we?"

It was shortly after 1994. The first democratic elections had taken place months earlier. Their family awoke early enough on that day to watch the sun rise as they readied themselves for their first election. The day had all the finery and ritual of a family outing rather than a day at the polls: their clothes had been carefully chosen, neat, if not formal. Shoes were polished, make-up applied, hair tidied and skirts arranged. Bart percolated coffee and stored this in a thermos. Lena filled an old ice-cream tub with sandwiches and placed these in a basket beside the flask – egg and mayonnaise on some, tuna on others. The meal came in handy as they stood in a thick line, personalities and outfits dissolving into one thing, the crowd advancing slowly towards the electoral box. Even so, there was the taste of euphoria as men and women, some so ancient that they could barely walk or see or hear, cast their ballots for the first time. Even when the rain came down the slow shuffle forward persisted, a patchwork of humanity beneath their umbrellas as the crowd waited. And waited. But then, democracy and freedom, come after decades of struggle, were worth the wait, and Zara, despite being two years shy of voting, remained beside her parents, not about to miss history in the making. Eventually, of course, the day receded into memory and Lena became the sceptic again. She claimed to distrust those who had negotiated the new country, and anyway, her politics and allegiances were not the same as that of the judge and the new ruling party. Instead, Lena used to hole up with other teachers discussing socialism, education, non-racism and the mechanics of changing the country fundamentally through the economy. They were opposed to compromise of any sort. "No," Lena had said, "souls cannot be bought like cakes at a sale ... and anyway, it will all go wrong eventually".

At the time of the invitation to meet James Ndlovu and his wife for tea, Zara had assumed that her mother's objections were political, ideological – it was an era in which friendships could be made or broken on the back of party affiliation. And, given that the judge had been a recent appointment to government as a senior counsel, she had always assumed that her mother's objections were about the judge and his politics.

"At some point I have to see him, Lena," Bart said, standing before them on the day of the judge's invitation, so that Zara could now, almost twenty years later, hear the quiet pleading.

They drove their orange *Volksie* to the city's smartest hotel. It was all English colonial, with high archways, plantation shutters and rolling lawns. As their car spluttered through the entrance, plumes of yellow smoke ushering them in, porters in pith helmets stood to attention at the gates and saluted.

"Good God ..." Lena sighed beneath her breath.

How displaced they must have looked. Her father in bus-conductor green pants, trying to disappear into the ground as they walked towards the dining hall. Lena proud wherever she went, in the way that someone who was determined not to be stymied by wealth or any sort of privilege was, and Zara, straggling behind with two plaits and a sundress. Or, no, she was a teenager by then, so perhaps it was a pair of jeans and a t-shirt that read: "This is not America" with a map of Africa beneath.

Their collective discomfort was palpable as the judge's lovely wife, Ma Ndlovu, regal in African skirts and a head wrap, poured tea.

They were an anomaly: the new order. The maids (what else could one call them, Zara thought, in their black dresses and white pinafores) were embarrassed, worse, mortified to serve them. People too much like themselves.

Still, the two families took tea on the terrace.

"Well, how nice that you came to join us," Ma Ndlovu said.

"Thank you ... " replied Lena graciously, charmed by the older woman's warmth despite her reservations.

But the rest of the meal was an awkward affair: pretending that this was what one did – one took tea on the terrace. The women pretending that their hearts were not shrivelling, their courage not faltering beneath the kind and unkind gazes of their fellow diners.

All the while the judge and her father tried to make small talk when quite clearly, Zara only now understood, more had been brewing than tea.

"Are you still teaching?" the judge asked Bart.

"I retired."

"You don't miss law?"

"No."

Was this all that Bart had said? Yet what a word to have travelled through the afternoon air and twenty years on.

"You should consider reopening those dusty law books – volunteer at a legal centre perhaps. Act as an advisor even. The country has moved on, so should you," the judge said, staring intently at Bart.

Had those been the judge's words? Perhaps, or something like that. Zara was watching her mother tuck delicately into a scone piled with cream, strawberry jam drifting down her chin. Lena with her beautiful bones and her inky black hair froze mid-bite, returned the scone to its plate and left it there to gather flies for the rest of the afternoon.

Zara realised, so many years later and so far away, that the aggrieved person in that room had been the judge. Not her father. Hadn't Bart bowed and virtually scraped the ground with his face in shame?

Her mother had not been reluctant to see the judge because of who he was, but because of what Bart had done. It all made immense, terrible sense. Bart had quit law to teach. Zara knew nothing else about his life until he met Lena, and now that she had looked, she saw that she had borne witness to something, a betrayal, possibly of Bart's best friend.

And Lena had known all about it.

23

When Ling's friend Michael called to say that he'd enjoyed meeting Zara and had asked whether she'd like to meet up for dinner that weekend in New Jersey, her intention had been to say no. Then how had she answered yes?

The dinner in a Turkish restaurant down on Bloomfield Avenue would later remind Zara about an article she had once read in a gossipy magazine: Point number 5: Never take a first date to a restaurant that you've not eaten at before (this after NEVER sleep with him on the first date, do NOT order anything with garlic or onions, do NOT wear anything too revealing, and, ONLY make small talk – no politics or religion, and definitely NO marriage).

Their conversation drifted to the presidential election.

"Look, I'm not saying he won't win ... but the odds are stacked ..." Michael began.

"And if he does? What does that say then?" enquired Zara.

"That a significant, and to my mind unexpected, shift in the psyche of the broader American consciousness has taken place ... when it comes to race, at least."

And then there was the talk of marriage. Michael saying this was not high on his list of priorities.

"My parents married young. And they always seemed twisted up with regret, perhaps because they believed they had missed out on some aspect of their own lives. But then, all my friends' parents were divorced, like, what, forty something or nearly fifty percent of Americans? So, no, I am not a proponent of marriage."

Zara sat silently through this. Because when she thought about it, she did not dislike the idea of marriage: two people bringing their lives together. And angry as she increasingly was with both her parents, their union had been oddly beautiful. There were times of awful conflict, mostly brought on by Lena's moods, Zara had begun to recall of late. But then there had also been love. Intense and enduring, which was all one could ever hope for surely. The way her father had nursed her mother through years of illness. His reminiscences of Lena long after her death, always heartfelt and hungry. And then, of course, there was Lena's shielding of whatever it was that Bart *had* done. They had always been together, a couple in the true sense, who still held hands despite the fact that their grown child looked away in disgust; a *pair* who spoke words that were beyond the rest of the world's understanding.

Lena certainly had had Bart's back. Whatever it was that she knew, she had accepted. After all, she had stayed, and a woman of her boldness and resolve might very well have left had she wanted to.

After the meal, which was bad and expensive, they walked to Zara's small flat, Michael complaining loudly about the restaurant not being to New York standards despite being thirty minutes from the city, and Zara blindly allowing the evening to run away from her. "So, who *are* you Zara Black?" Michael asked, as he leaned on her bed, his long legs rearranging the sense that this was still her quiet room. He had riffled through the pile of CDs atop her suitcase and selected something by Nina Simone.

"Historian. South African. Cousin," she answered, surprised by the fact that she had eliminated "orphan" from this description. "You?"

"A writer in the first instance. Beyond that it's all still a crap shoot," he answered, wrapping her hair around his finger.

The air was so thick with it, the conversation so geared towards what happened next that Zara could hardly claim later that she had not designed it.

The sex was slow and gentle; Michael held her, cupping her face in his hands as he kissed her. It was reassuring to be held, to feel a part of someone, yet the intimacy unearthed all kinds of sordid emotions within her.

Once Michael left the following morning, after an uneasy sleep for Zara, she climbed into the shower, allowed the water to run hard against her body and face as she tried to scrub away all the lies.

Perhaps the brutal honesty of flesh against her own, the unblemished bareness of sharing a single bed with a man she barely knew, had allowed her to accept truths that she had not previously acknowledged: like what almighty crackpots her parents, her mother especially, had been.

Now, the memories were drowning Zara: her mother's migraines, and let-mummy-just-sleep-a-little-while days and the times she had been posted to her grandmother so that her mother could sit on the couch and stare at the walls or paint morose pictures of boats tossing at sea.

If Zara had to diagnose her parents (as it turned out she *had* to), then she would have to describe her father as pathologically self-deprecating and her mother Lena as chronically depressed, at worst, bi-polar. *This* revelation that Lena was not a seventies ideal of love, peace and harmony after all, came surprisingly as a shock.

*

Lena's Indian father had been a Christian convert whose zealousness for his adopted faith saw him cross an ocean, and soon he had found himself in Cape Town.

Apparently, by Lena's reckoning, he had taken one look at the sea, mountain and forests. He had smelled the honeysuckle growing wild in the front yard of the church he had come to work in, remembered the strife and hunger and clawing heat he had left behind, and decided that the city would be his new home. Soon he'd found a Cape Town woman who would have him – a woman who it was believed had her own secrets (the family rumour being that she had been Muslim and somehow turned against her faith, or, perhaps, that it had turned against her). So Zara's grandmother came without family, without even an allusion to family. Nonetheless, eight children later, Lena was born.

The story continued until Lena's parents, nine children in tow, found themselves living on the church's property, somewhere between the ocean and the train track. The family entertainment: catching potential converts as they stretched their legs for the fifteen minutes that the train stopped at their station.

Lena's father would invite whomever seemed most amiable to his charms to view the church's prized rose garden. He would insist that if the traveller had their belongings with them (for safety) then why miss an incredible sight: a rose in the softest shade of lavender that he had himself cultivated. Anyway, he'd add convincingly, the whole expedition wouldn't take more than a few minutes. Duly, the strangers would follow this kindly holy man with the curious accent. But, once caught up in the wonder of that garden, lovingly tended, the train would depart leaving the travellers stranded until the next train, two hours later. Just then, Lena's mother would bring out the cake and tea and children, as her father began his persuasion and attempt at conversion: gently at first, cajoling, even arguing if he had to, in order to get one more bell ringing in heaven.

According to Lena, standing behind the station pelting stones at the train and watching this drama day after day, she would never be convinced of the kindness of strangers or the sanctity of the church again.

Still, it had been an idyllic childhood growing up beside the ocean, and Lena spent her first years thinking of life beside the beach as a perfectly natural and normal thing. When her family was forced out of their home by the government of the day, and redirected to suburbs which did not have views of the ocean or mountains, perhaps something came loose in Lena, and the rebel's path was chosen.

The house that Lena, Bart and Zara lived in was compact.

"No more than a family of your station might need." Lena repeated the housing official's words for decades thereafter.

"Yes ... of course, I suppose you would think that," she began slowly. "But you see, from what I have seen, only hard work, kindness or intelligence really separates one person from the other." She stared back as few would have dared. "But given how long you have taken to process this simple form," she said, raising her index finger to eye level, "your swallowing of an ideology you've been taught without question," two, her fingers indicated, "and your thoughtless words just this minute," three, "I would say you are not qualified to judge me." She picked up the forms from the counter, and marched out with her head straining ridiculously high above her neck.

The garden of their home on that long dry street was no more than a flat wasteland of weeds and daisy bushes that sprang up every summer, despite the fact that no one tended them or longed for them during the cold or cared that they had even managed to show up again. The lone tree that had started its life in that garden had been unceremoniously uprooted by Lena one day soon after her blue mood gave way to a fury at everything that was ugly and wrong about the place. The alien species, Lena, teacher of biology and science at a local high school, informed her incredulous neighbours, had no business in her garden or anywhere on the African continent. No, it would have to live elsewhere, she said, depositing the tree – which, despite its crime, was wrapped gently in wet towels – at the council's local offices.

Zara didn't know whether it was her mother's opposition to the city council's attempts at beautification that set them apart from other families on that long, dry road. Or whether it was the way their washing hung on the line for days at a time – through showers and sunshine and wind and back through another onset of showers before anyone in the family seemed to realize that they had hung washing out there at all. Shy and contained, Zara never could make a single friend on that street for all the years she lived there; but then she had been born between two extremities – parents of hot and cold, vigour and apathy, mayhem and order – and because of this, was forced into a neutral position at a young age and duly learned, as all children of kooks inevitably must, to walk the middle road. This left her uninspiring to her peers. On top of her often-corrected English that came out too taut, her reserve kept her standing to the side, watching metal cans being kicked across the road.

It was under Lena's tutelage that Zara learned to lambast lies and secrets and obfuscation of any sort. Lena had always advocated transparency in everything, which was why she said she couldn't trust the new government – what deals had been signed and compromises made to jump so effortlessly from oppressed to liberator? There had been no revolution, no truth of blood to secure a new order. Lena hated misrepresentations, slander, sleight-of-hands, and you could add small talk to that too. No, what Lena had believed her own childhood had taught her, and what life had certainly confirmed was the necessity of truth.

Apparently not, Zara decided, stepping out of the shower and leaving behind the filth not only of her parents' lies, but her blindness to what had been happening all around her; her own deceptions too.

24

Lena rotated on her own axis, much like the two other residents who lived in that house on the long dry road. She was a restless spirit, capable of swinging between admiring a flower to demanding obedience to the revolution. Even her cooking had to be dealt with, sending smoke signals up and down their street, relating in great detail to their neighbours what the Blacks would eat for dinner. Zara, though, knew her mother's secret: Lena took pleasure in not being able to conjure a decent meal. She wilfully burned eggs as she read; an indication perhaps of larger preoccupations, of a mind trained on the world.

Still, Lena was caught out by her own loyalties. Her child had to be fed. Her husband could or would not cook every night. She did what she had to do. The food of her choice: her Indian father's cuisine.

Like his daughter, Lena's father had been conflicted; while he wished to be seen as a Western man in his ill-fitting second hand suits, he could do nothing but eat the cuisine of his heart. Indian peasant food he had called it: dal and rice, dosas filled out with curried potato, beans cooked in masala, garlic and ginger and the contents of any number of unnamed redolent bags of spice. It was these recipes that Lena mangled and rewrote according to her own skill.

To be in the kitchen with her *had* felt to Zara like being in the middle of a whirlwind:

"Well, what's the point? The point ... I wanted to know ..." Lena was stirring up some concoction that day, the smell of burned turmeric scalding the late afternoon air, "... why teach if I cannot explain the broader context, life, the world at large ... don't introduce politics, he says ... science is pure ... he says," Lena was at her most animated as Zara sat at the counter, ignoring her school books in favour of the live action in their kitchen. "Science is pure, he says ... well, my left leg to that. So I said ... Zara, that is the wrong answer, Hamlet, not Macbeth ... I said to this school inspector: your science insists we are an inferior species, so your science, I'd say, has introduced politics already ... well, I can tell you he didn't like that. No, not Inspector Van der Westhuizen. Him and his sidekick nose, hanging on his face like ... well, I blushed ..." she said, as Zara watched her mother closely.

Lena's politics were no less conciliatory than her cooking. Her friends were a mismatched bunch of teachers, who self- identified as revolutionaries. Lenin and Marx they believed in, while Stalin they pointedly insisted was a tyrant, a dictator, no worse, a brutal murderer, who had corrupted socialism. To add to that, they were firm that his ideas had contaminated local struggle politics.

"Unity is the ideal, after all. But really, how can we stand by and support Stalinism – the man was a brute, my God aside from the millions, he murdered Trotsky!" they all sighed in acknowledgment, "Trotsky, and the lives of three of his children under Stalin's boot!"

This strange world of dead Russian men intrigued Zara, and she recalled asking in all her naivety, "I don't get it, why the big conflict here?"

"In life those two were enemies. They disagreed fundamentally. We pick up the swords a million miles away, decades later …"

From what Zara observed, the group's arguments over politics, however heated, usually rose above the clinking of tea cups. The battle, sounding near, felt further afield. And when the occasional teacher was arrested, Zara was certain that the news would be accompanied by equal amounts of horror and enthusiasm. But the quick release of their colleague and comrade confirmed that the teachers were not any great threat to the police after all.

Still, when Lena spoke, it was about "us" and "we" – not as it pertained to royalty, but as it did to the revolution. We, the people. The words had a strange effect on Zara – making her feel slightly bigger than herself. As if the walls of their home at the end of that long dry street were not quite as tight as they usually seemed.

Bart only ever skulked around as Lena spoke or cooked, cautioning his wife not to add too much of this or that.

"Stomach like a kitten," Lena would complain in return, as Bart followed instructions to make himself useful elsewhere. He never attended her meetings. Nor did he raise his opinions in company, and only Lena and Zara knew his laments about the country. He didn't eat foods that disagreed with him. He took everything in his stride. Perhaps it was also this quality that made Bart seem so nice; ineffectual perhaps, but nice all the same. And perhaps a little pathetic?

One evening in their kitchen, Zara's father recalled his days at university. He mentioned Judge Ndlovu, and a woman's name – the first time Zara had heard it: Marybeth, barely mumbled.

Lena stopped doing whatever she had been busy with. Deliberately, she rested a hand on the freshly peeled pair of onions lying head to head on the wooden cutting board. She raised one to her lips and sank her teeth deep into its flesh, chewing until her face was awash with tears.

"No ... no ... don't upset yourself now Lena ... I was just wanting to tell Sha Sha a story ..." Bart tried to placate her.

But Lena stalked to the bedroom, slamming the door shut behind her. Zara was left seated at the kitchen counter, her father trying to find words or an explanation. Instead, he walked into the lounge, and only when Zara heard his music emanating from the Hi-fi system, did she make herself a sandwich for dinner before retreating into her books.

*

What could Zara, so many years later, make of her mother's onion-eating rages, or her father's helplessness?

Perhaps, that Bart had been diminished by Lena, while her mother had been as far gone as a kite without string.

Zara shut down her laptop. It was ten p.m. Too early to let the last of summer's evenings slip by. Zara stretched, took a minute to think it through before she grabbed a jacket, ran downstairs and out of 780 on Bloomfield. *This* was a memory in her bones. Only, it wasn't her memory, but that of her mother.

Lena: tying on a fading pair of takkies and heading towards the door late in the evening, a sign that she had fallen down the rabbit hole.

"Lena you can't go for a walk now ... what are you thinking ... those gangsters won't hesitate to drag you into some corner," Bart would have said, as he stood at the door nervously trying to hold his wife with words. "Zara won't be able to sleep until you are back," he would have called out desperately, as Lena reached the gate, anticipating that this, if anything, would slow her down. Despite her troubles, Lena had been a loving mother. What Zara remembered was this: lying with her cheek pressed deep into her mother's own; her smell, which was not patchouli after all, but something cleaner and simpler, perhaps laundry detergent underpinned by a floral fragrance. Lena had been Zara's world: she had listened patiently to essays being read, questions being rehearsed, exam papers being dissected. Lena, though, had not known where too far was, and often required supervision herself. If not discouraged, Lena would have stayed home to nurse Zara's illnesses, walked up and down with boxes of tissues and glasses of orange juice until she fell ill herself, or, warned off teachers who raised a ruler in Zara's direction.

Zara stopped walking when she spotted a metal gate behind which someone had taken great care in cultivating a hothouse vegetable garden. In the middle of the suburbs of a town in Northern New Jersey, she could see through the slit of the fence carrots, herbs, lettuce, growing and flourishing even in the torrid summer months of the East Coast. Zara smiled.

Then her phone rang.

"Hello?" She had avoided the last few calls from Michael. It had all happened too soon – and all the revelations that Michael had unwittingly released had been too much. Still, and despite herself, Zara hoped it might be him.

"Zara? Can you hear me?" Amy's voice came across the distance.

"Amy, hi! I can hear you," Zara said, making her way to the pavement. "Are you alright?"

"Zee, I wanted to let you know before you read it. A journalist friend just called me. Something is going down here. There's lots of talk about settling scores and some sort of a witch hunt ... names of spies being released ... it will happen soon Zee, and I've heard your dad's name is on the list ... Zee? Did you hear me? They're releasing ..."

"Yes, I heard you Amy. When?" Zara asked impatiently.

"No, I don't know that ... are you ok?"

"What exactly have you heard Amy?"

"Just that names would be released and that there was someone with the name Black on it, Zee. I don't know anything else. Are you alright?"

"I'll be ok. Yes, I'm fine. Look, I have to go, but I'll call you in a few days, ok?" Zara said thickly, and hung up. She stood up from where she had been hunched on the pavement and began to make her way home.

25

When the news came, almost one year had passed since Zara had left home.

There was no toll of doom that sounded, no rattling in her bones and no deciphering of monsters in the day sky: nothing dramatic at all.

A new invitation from Judge Ndlovu to meet at his hotel came a day later, after the call from Amy, when Zara was seated at her desk, distracted, but in conversation with Ling.

"Do you like these?" Ling pointed down to her newest acquisition of shoes.

"Urm ... no, not really ... can't say I do," Zara had replied, barely bothering to look up, as she tried to scan the internet for news.

"Why not?"

"It's just not my style, Ling. Too ... too ... flashy for campus. They're gold," Zara answered, glancing quickly at what Ling was inspecting closely. "Better for after five in the evening, I think."

"What? Where is this handbook on style that you keep scoring me on? After five ... see, those are Jersey rules. In Manhattan, never would you hear such a thing ..."

"You asked my opinion," Zara continued, her eyes never straying from the screen.

"Yes, I certainly did that ..."

Their morning conversation had wound down when her phone rang.

"Yes, hi …" Zara answered quickly, aware that her manner was becoming more economical, more American on the phone.

It was Judge Ndlovu and he wanted to see her. Could she come immediately?

"I have been trying to reach you … did you get my messages? I sent several emails … but right now I am at work. Do you think it could wait until this evening?" Zara asked brusquely.

"Zara, I know I haven't made time to speak to you before, but what I have to tell you really cannot wait. Tonight will be too late. Please …"

"Well … I suppose I can make up for lost time here … If I leave now I can be there in an hour or so …" Zara said, and shut down her laptop, knocking over her coffee cup as she did so.

Ling looked up at the commotion. "What is it?"

"That was an old friend of my dad's. It's urgent," Zara added, as she wiped away the mess and cleared her desk.

*

Zara made her way to the same hotel and up to the suite in which the judge was staying. The door was angled inwards, so that she caught sight of the judge seated at the desk before his laptop, his forehead resting in his hand.

"Judge …" Zara said, pushing the door open.

"Please, come inside," he said, without rising to greet her this time.

She found a place on the couch facing him, and turned so that he would have her full attention.

"Would you like anything? Some coffee or tea perhaps?" he asked listlessly.

"No, thank you. I'd like to know what's going on. Why you have avoided me for all these months and then suddenly ..."

"Yes, I know Zara. I know."

He shut down his computer. Shifted his pen from one side to the other, laid it down one way, then another, until he settled on arranging it perpendicularly to his laptop.

"Tomorrow a list of names will be released. Now this list is not about justice, or freedom of information, no matter what you hear," he said, as his eyes remained focussed ahead of him, while his hands tried to quell his unease. "It will be about moving the pieces about on the board ... a balancing of forces. Someone with a great deal of power wants someone else out of the way. And this, this last resort – the roll of shame - the one we thought would never be used, has been ... unfurled," he enunciated the word slowly.

"Will my father's name be on this list?"

"Yes. But I believe his name is incidental; the bigger name, well ... that is there too, and the real reason for all of this. It has nothing to do with Bart. But of course to you ... I want you to know what he stands accused of before you read it elsewhere."

"What will this list say he did?" Zara asked tightly.

He stood up, walked to the window without looking out, and then just as suddenly he returned to the desk and took his place again.

"You see, Zara, when we met, I have told you, your father was one of a handful of people who I could call a friend. I mean a real friend: not someone who associated with me at university but who would not sit beside me at the canteen or refuse to greet me in the street. There were many like that. Not Bart. He never thought the differences between us to be significant: what we looked like, what we ate, wore, who we worshipped. This is what set him apart."

"Yes, I know all of this."

He raised his hand weakly as if it were a white flag. A note of defeat. There would be no more secrets.

"We were a trio – did you know? Your father, me, and Marybeth Harrison. Have you heard her name?"

"I know she was in a relationship with my father. I don't think I was meant to know. The things that aren't said, well, we know them anyway ... but what does this have to do with you summoning me?" The word did not quite slip out.

"Have I summoned you? Is that what I've done Zara?" the judge asked, injured.

"It felt that way."

"We were never meant to become ... people who summon," he said. "People who sell out their old comrades to wage political battles, to score political points. Or ... or ..." he began searching the air, "When we were young what we were focused on was victory. We sacrificed a great deal and what mattered was freedom: a light at the end of a long tunnel. I realise now that we didn't think carefully enough about how we must approach this freedom. What we should expect. What we should do when we arrive at that place; and how we must adjust. Who and how we will sacrifice ..."

"Judge, what are you talking about? What are you saying?" Zara walked closer to him.

"When Marybeth left Bart, she came to me."

"When? What do you mean?"

"It's the oldest of stories," he said, looking at her with weary eyes. "She and I were always more alike, driven by this desire to fight the regime, and we did. But us ... the idea of it was almost unheard of back then: a rural black man and a white woman, even amongst our own comrades. But it was inevitable and after a while, well, she and I we became ... you know, more than friends. He found out. He must have. And then ... I don't know Zara, how do I tell you this – it was him. He gave us up. There was no torture, he wasn't even arrested." Judge Ndlovu buried his head in his hands. "Some madness befell Bart, and one day he rose off the couch after Marybeth had come back from a trip to Johannesburg. After she had been with me and somehow he knew. He must always have known. He walked out the door and hours later the police arrived. He watched them take her away."

"How do you know it was him? It could have been anyone, it was well known that she was an activist, that just by them living together they were flouting the Immorality Act ..."

"Zara, it was him. They knew details that Marybeth said only he and she knew about her political work. It was Bart."

Zara sat on the couch, trying to comprehend all that she had heard.

"So you see, one betrayal followed another. But of course," he said, it seemed, to himself, "everyone has a story of some betrayal: sold out for political beliefs by a friend ... betrayed by your country because you were sent off to fight a war which you didn't comprehend, fellow citizens who looked the other way when you were being arrested, tortured ... and now ... old friends ..." He was rambling, words tumbling over each other.

"Is your name on the list?" Zara asked quietly.

"My name is the one that matters most on this list. I have angered someone very high up. I have said too much. Differed once too often. You see, in the past dissent was perceived as something dangerous; it could have crippled the entire movement. And now?" he said, looking at Zara pleadingly, "the same rules seem to apply, as if we are still fighting the old battles, Zara." He stood up, but sat back down at once.

He began calmly again, "All I can tell you with certainty is that I have made too many rulings which are disliked by those that matter. Just rulings, but it seems that is not what counts ..."

"Tell me what happened to her ..." Zara asked, as she dusted the couch of a strand of errant light.

"It was her torture that broke me. *That*. That idea. I didn't care then if she spoke. I hoped that she would. That she would sell me out if her life were at stake. First they arrested her, then they swooped on several of us and I was arrested with many others. To save her I would have said anything. There was no question. After two months she was released, then one by one the rest of us, and somehow she made her way out of the country. Hha!" a hollow cry echoed from his lips. "She would have nothing to do with me when she found out that I had spoken. I told them where we met, what we discussed ... you see Zara I did it because I couldn't bear to hear them say her name, what they said they would do. But to her, I'd been weakened, compromised. I never saw her again; she moved first to England and then next I heard she was in Canada, married to a doctor, Shuster, or no, he was Schusler. She died before she could return home." He stood up, walked to the window and looked at the park, green and pure in the afternoon sun. When he spoke it was another man's voice that Zara heard. "So you see, the betrayals, they pile up on each other. One for one, against and above the other. Our country's museum of loss, our killing fields, aren't filled with corpses, even if the bodies are there. No, our museum is populated with betrayals, stacked sky high."

26

Outside, the light was already starting to fade. Zara walked.

An old man stood at the corner selling hotdogs from a cart: his vertically striped baseball sweater and the peak cap resting on his head making it seem that he had been there, selling his hotdogs with ketchup, or mustard, or the works, or with a pickle bursting with joy, for decades. He smiled as she walked past, the almost imperceptible nod of his head, a greeting. The clothing store that he sold his wares in front of had been fashioned, Zara gathered, to look older than it was. The sign on which the store's name appeared, *Clarissa's*, had been distressed, yellow paint worn to beige, the door and frame a mere memory of white as she walked by. Perhaps the hot-dog seller had been standing there for fifty years after all. She walked on, past a taxi reversing erratically at the corner, the driver's eyes grazing hers momentarily as he revved the engine.

Zara focussed on the striding of her legs as they brushed past each other, the slapping of her shoes as she tried to overtake the man ahead of her with the Blackberry to his ear. She watched with great interest as the pavement dissected into a grid of blocks, first vertical then horizontal, her feet moving between joints and cracks on the pavement as she made her way down the street. It was a wonder to Zara that American roads could be so very long. She had walked early one morning all the way down Bloomfield Avenue to get out of her apartment. For two hours she'd walked without stopping, and still did not find the end of that road. She had strode past lavish houses that covered two or three properties with their six bedrooms, three reception rooms, pools that froze in winter, and the occasional stable. Zara had tried to catch a glimpse of the women who drove out of these driveways from houses that could barely be seen from the road. But they were too fast and high in their urban tanks. Eventually, Zara had stopped at a high school on the edge of town; catching her breath for only five minutes, she'd begun the two-hour journey back.

In the City that evening, Zara only slowed at red lights, neither stopping nor hesitating, she moved between cars and taxis at pause. Inspecting the trite details of buildings, she made herself into a tourist for a few minutes: how many windows this one had, how long and gothic that one was. How had she never before noticed that elongated building with the flourish at its crown?

But eventually, Zara had to stop: out of breath, she stood and looked around. She was Downtown. Close to Bleecker. The street lights had gone on. The roads were dark and the city had taken on another mood. She could hear laughter, music starting up somewhere, orders being shouted inside a restaurant. Zara joined the line at some café, lacking the conviction required for queuing, but uncertain of what else to do with her legs, she waited. Only when she was seated at the counter, an unwanted coffee before her, did Zara ask for a take away instead, making her way to an empty bench in a nearby park.

She had been expelled from her own life, from her own memory of her mother and the legacy of her father as a dispassionate man.

As it turned out, her father had indeed been capable of passion and a strain of it that ate away at his own life, and deep into her own.

The full cup of coffee discarded, Zara evaluated her hands. Placing the weight of shame of her father in one and the judge's in the other, she made a study of her empty palms. But then, how could these deceptions ever be balanced? After all, had the betrayal of a comrade to the police, certainly without duress, not been amongst the most hateful of deeds during the struggle? Unforgiveable? They had been his closest friends. To add to this was the idea that Bart had never absolved himself, had never come clean. And then what of the judge's deceptions: against Bart, and those against his comrades – were they any nobler because they sought to save his lover? Marybeth certainly hadn't thought so.

But the big question for Zara was this: had she known? Had Lena known all along? But of course she must have. Had Lena not thought to leave her daughter a hint of what might possibly come: the trail of deception that would litter Zara's path, rendering it impassable?

*

In the days that followed, Zara moved into the library with her laptop and coffee in a flask that she drank from when the librarians were in some otherworldly zone of the building – the compactus or the dim basement. She realised that she was subtracting herself from Ling and Michael and her work, and certainly from what she had learned about her father; but she felt strong enough to do only this.

Starting early each day, she worked her way methodically through an entire wall of the Africa Library's South Africa section: skimming or reading fully when the library was quiet – searching for what, she could not say.

That side fiction, over here non-fiction. She ran her hand across the titles pulling out the ones which interested her, and amongst these found biographies, autobiographies, historical accounts, textbooks, journals and diaries, all confirming a growing genre of betrayal, spawned since the end of apartheid. She flipped through these books, memorised titles to which she would return.

In the black broad files were documents, analysis and interpretations of TRC testimonies beside soft cover books with newspaper clippings about the trials. She sat with these for days. Reading in full the testimonies on the internet when she felt brave enough.

Maybe the judge was correct, and right here was a small piece of the museum: a place for artefacts and matters of national importance, a monument to the past, or perhaps, a place for memory and healing. Perhaps even for that American idea: closure, and books to help bring it about.

Zara stayed in the fiction section for days. She carried heaps of books to the desk closest to the window, so that she could watch the campus settle into evening. Electric lights blinking against layers of night sky.

"You alright, Ma'am?" a young student assistant was standing before her. His pale hair falling over one eye only. Offering her what? Assistance? A book? Or was he curious about why she had been there night after night? Ma'am. How that word grated.

"I'm alright, thanks," Zara answered, but before he could walk away, she stopped him: "Do you read?"

"I'm sorry Ma'am, I don't understand the question."

"Fiction, do you read?" She motioned to the summit in front of her.

"Sure," he said, looking at her with a puzzled expression. He had passed by her several times in the last few evenings after he'd come on duty, returning books to their shelves or searching for a volume that was due to be collected, a pink slip of paper held between his fingers.

"What?"

"I'm sorry, Ma'am?"

"What books do you read? And my name is Zara," she said, smiling faintly.

"Oh, whatever is around," he answered, straightening his grey t-shirt and pushing the straw hair out of his eye. "I like science fiction. But, right now I'm reading Faulkner. It's part of my course work."

"Would you read it otherwise?"

He took a moment: "Yeah, I guess I would actually. I probably would," he replied, pushing the hair back again and blushing faintly.

"Does it matter? I mean does it make any difference to you? If you were to never have encountered it, Faulkner I mean, would it have made a difference?" Zara asked, and she noted that he had started to tug at his t-shirt. She was scaring the polite, well-raised young man.

"Probably ... I mean sure, it matters. It's about us, right?" he said, before moving off hurriedly, holding on as the pink slip carried him down the corridor and away from the crazy lady sitting in African Fiction.

Zara looked at the growing list before her: multi-generational epics, sagas with recipes inside of them filled with belated history, self discovery, questions of identity, writings of the past as it had never been previously written. The crime fiction collection covered three shelves. More stories of betrayal and others of absolution. Some books were clean of the past: romances, family epics where the past had been another place entirely, or volumes of the futuristic and supernatural. If it were at all possible, this was where Zara would wish her story to be. Yes, here was where she would locate herself, if only she could.

But of course, she could not.

27

It was after fifteen years in their small house that Bart finally relented and agreed that they should move to the family home on the hill with his mother.

This debate had taken place on many afternoons.

"It's all so mean. So mean and ... and petty. Look at that little ridiculous garden. Really ... how do we have dignity when this place defies it?" Lena might have begun years earlier, walking in from outside and exclaiming, "Why can't we just move in with your mother Bart? It is your house after all, your father left it to you for Christ's sake!" Lena's anger was always sudden and rushed through the house.

"Lena, please, we have had this discussion. I will not live in my father's house. You know the reasons ..."

"Ancient history. Yes, your father betrayed his mother, you've said a million times, but the house stands there, large and empty with just your mother. She might not even notice if we moved in. Please, please, let's leave this soulless place?" her voice soon pleading as Zara held her breath.

"Lena, please. If we move there after all these years of saying we will not accept the fruits of my father's deceits, then all these years here in this house were pointless ..."

"Now it *is* pointless," Lena's voice was steel. "The man is dead. You are making a point to a dead man. What you are really doing is inflicting suffering on yourself for your father's sins. Suffering for the sake of suffering. But what you don't see is that everyone in this country has some guilt for something they've done somewhere along the line; so your ethics, your dignities are quite insignificant and missing the mark ..." she said, leaving the room. Her exits were always followed by clambering and cluttering until Lena surfaced minutes later with her canvases, paints, brushes and her own silence in retaliation for Bart's many over the years.

One day they did move though. When Zara's grandmother Hannah was already in her nineties. She was "on her last", as Zara's aunts repeatedly said. This left Zara with the distinct and terrible impression that every meal would be Hannah's final supper, every excursion to the toilet might result in calamity behind the bathroom door, and at the end of every breath she might turn blue. Zara and Amy, teenage girls then, were Hannah's line of defence against irritable daughters who, in all fairness, had been ignored for the better part of their lives, for the better loved son, Bart. The teenagers slept at the house every opportunity they got – as if this would somehow hold off the inevitable.

It was then that the Black sisters decided that Bart's duty had finally fallen to him. He would have to move into *his* house to look after *his* mother. As Hannah lay on her death bed her children squabbled in the lounge:

"You see Bart, I can't manage all of this, I have my own house, my family. I haven't been able to manage for years. And Daddy left this blessed house to you, anyway. So you must decide now. What will happen to mother and the house?" said Emma, Bart's elder sister, as she brushed bits of cake from her cheek to her chin and rearranged her body beneath a forgiving blue pinafore.

"I never wanted this place ..." Bart began, but resigned himself to silence instead.

Rose, ears everywhere, hissed over Emma's shoulder. "The house is yours, so either you must sell and send your mother to an old-age home, or, you and your family move in. Are those crumbs on your chin, Emmie?" Rose asked without even a hint of sweetness.

"It's time now, Bart," Emma said, and motioned to Lena.

"Yes ..." Bart agreed, watching his beautiful, doomed wife. Lena had been diagnosed, and had lost a breast. She had battled radiation therapy, a procession of doctors and specialists, pitying colleagues and curious students. But she had been unfailingly brave, of course. Lena had been victorious. But all of that would change.

They moved into the old house at the top of a hill where Hannah's roses continued to bloom until she died. Peacefully, everyone insisted. Only Zara and Amy doubted that death could ever be serene, violent as a last breath surely was.

In the two summers that followed, it rained almost non-stop. Zara and Lena tended Hannah's garden.

"She would have liked the idea of us gardening on her behalf ... but that wind ..." Lena said, patting the earth with her bare hands, as she stared at the folds of white cloud falling down the mountain.

Zara had felt something akin to happiness then; perhaps the only time she ever had. Or maybe the ebbing of Lena's moods, placated as she was by the ocean before them, or the mountain behind them, had calmed them all. Even Bart seemed less anxious, less liable to apologise for his very presence in those two years before the return of Lena's cancer.

At least, Zara decided, at least, she had those years.

28

The day after Judge Ndlovu returned to South Africa, after the names had been released, a phalanx of reporters greeted him on his arrival in Johannesburg. The images of the judge walking through the airport, his head held low and his clothes crumpled, dishevelled after the twenty-two hour flight, were in contrast to the reel Zara had playing in her head: of the boy made good who had travelled by train to Cape Town, graduated at the top of his class, who wore fine clothes, had mastered a second language, and was amongst the most respected of legal opinions. Perhaps, after all, he was just a man.

The photos made every local paper from what Zara could surmise, with one printed in black and white on page four of the New York Times, beside a short article.

The noise about the judge only grew louder in the weeks that followed. Each day a new revelation about him became known: on Monday it was reported that the judge and his wife had once accepted a trip abroad, paid out of state coffers. By Tuesday the story was rebutted: it was a conference and the judge had reimbursed fully the cost of his wife's trip. By Wednesday rumours of a sexual harassment claim against him surfaced, buried by Thursday beneath strenuous denials by anonymous colleagues. It seemed everyone knew some detail of the man, and duly his life was dismembered into a million pieces.

Then the sudden press conference and the shock announcement of Judge Ndlovu's retirement. Zara found the recordings online and watched, her heart thudding along to his every word, listening for her father's name. It never came. The judge made his confession, if that was what it was, without implicating Bart. He offered no proof of his dedication to the country, and refused to provide any detailed explanation of the circumstances in which he had betrayed. All he gave fully were his apologies.

Still, the headlines persisted for days: *Judicial Witch Hunt, say Judges! Treason, say Youth! Traitor, agrees Minister S—.*

And then, just as suddenly, although it was not sudden at all, after months of infighting, the president of the country resigned. Fractures, which had been spreading beneath the surface, had finally risen. And the country waited.

The judge though, with his life scattered in pieces around his feet, vanished behind the seven-foot walls of his Sandton home. And Bart? His name disappeared, at least temporarily, along with the other hundred or so traitors, as they had become known.

Still, if there was an idea that Bart deserved absolution, it did not come from Zara. The shame itself seemed to be slowly settling on her skin. She did not believe that she could walk in the world knowing, as others did, that her father had done something unpardonable.

She had avoided Amy since the news had become known, emailing or texting only the most perfunctory messages. Zara was careful to steer clear of Ling and any questions about what was wrong and what had happened with Michael. She watched the phone ring on silent when Michael did call. It was too soon; the wrong time; it's not you it's me. What could she possibly say to Michael that would not sound trite and insincere?

The silence of her colleagues from home was proof enough that the news had reached the staid halls of academia. Zara could hear the susurration of wagging tongues across the Atlantic. How could she ever go back to deal with that or have her students watching her from beneath their brows: *Did you hear about her? Eish! I'd be like totally hu-mi-li-ated if that was my parent. To-tally!*

There was, as far as Zara could see, no antidote to shame. Nor could she see any reason to return home soon, or perhaps ever again.

29

There is an image that Zara could never wipe away, of Lena crawling on all fours in the dirt. At her happiest digging, planting and patting the soil with her bare hands, before sitting and nudging the sunhat back and away from her eyes with a garden fork so that she could assess her work. She could grow anything. A rose plant taken from a slip of nothing, a bushel of beans grown from a small dried legume found at the bottom of the kitchen cupboard, a row of flowers from an old packet of seeds. Under Lena's reign, there was no reading in the garden or afternoon tea in that old family home.

Lena tended the garden's flowers for the sake of Hannah's memory, but paid far more attention to her veggies and fruits, and what these might still become. She grew vegetables that could be picked and turned into homemade soups so that their cupboards filled with carrots and beans and peaches preserved in spices and vinegar or sugar. Not once did Lena laze in the sun as the lovely Black sisters had done so many decades before.

For Zara that had been a time of real happiness. An era of calm, and perhaps, also, the beginning of her love affair with the past. Theirs was a new country, where politics, even if momentarily, had mellowed and many were free to garden or read. After the years of struggle, it felt a time for self-indulgent pleasures, to think of "I" and not only "we".

That was the time Zara had begun to pay attention to her father. Evaluating him in something of a new light and finding him for the first time less than boring. Bart's music collection grew during those years. He erected a library stocked with long playing records of the greats: Davis, Ebrahim, Fitzgerald, Holiday. He only ever took one album out at a time from shelves that stretched along the walls of the room that had been Hannah's lounge. Gingerly, he would slip a record from its plastic sleeve, swivel it towards the light, blow dust from its wide black face before nudging away dirt with a cloth made of the softest leather. His collection of vinyl music made him interesting to Zara's school friends and boys she occasionally brought home.

In those days, before the full weight of Lena's illness set in, Zara could still persuade Bart into telling her about Isaiah. His story. About Kimberley. How he and Hannah had met; the origins of the surname Black.

"You mean we could very well be called Penny-Farthing, or Goldstein, or September for that matter?" Zara asked one evening.

"I'm not so sure," Bart said, a slight smile playing around his eyes, as he alphabetised his albums for the tenth time that week.

"There must be some birth record somewhere?"

"No. Isaiah was probably not even registered. Remember, it was a diamond mine, a camp – a different world. Hardly a country then."

"We are people without name ..." Zara mused as she ran her finger along the record shelves.

"We are people."

Zara must have been about sixteen, or seventeen then. All elbows and shoulders beneath a thicket of hair. Rebellious in a country that had decided to put rebelliousness aside. Still, what was it about hip hop that made her feel so radical? Her father hated it, her mother too. No matter, she couldn't shake the feeling that the world had been made just for her and her generation.

When Lena's illness returned, it was short and to the point and by the time she went to see a doctor she had months left to live. Months in which the cancer did not spare any of them their dignity or pride.

And when Lena's death came, it was shocking for the emptiness that remained in a place that had once been full and vital. Aside from this, her demise contained few surprises. Lena had planned and arranged her funeral down to the smallest detail. There would be nothing as depressing as an open casket – it should be sealed tight, with nails if need be. Furthermore, she would not have the hypocrisy of a post-funeral tea. She would have none of that "She was lovely, and such a good teacher nonsense," she'd said, her finger in the air, so that they would know she was deadly serious.

"No, I want wine, music, Oscar Wilde read – 'Death must be so beautiful. To lie in the soft brown earth, with the grasses waving above one's head, and listen to silence. To have no yesterday, and no to-morrow. To forget time, to forgive life, to be at peace'" Lena had said, a waver creeping into her voice. "No," she shook off the fear and bleak reality and began again, "let people say what they want. I want a celebration of life."

Even so, her assurances that her passing would be overcome, that it should be embraced for the time it had given them, did not convince either Bart or Zara. They knew, had always known, that when she was gone there would be nothing between them and the world.

On the day of the funeral a gothic fog that would have pleased Lena spread across the graveyard. In the end, Lena had relented, agreeing that there could be a grave, a service and tributes.
The graveyard was close to the ocean where Lena had grown up. Now that apartheid was a thing of the past, the suburb beside the sprawling Atlantic welcomed her back.

Bart and Zara, almost twenty, led the slow march from cars that had to be left on a small patch of grass outside the gate, as the party walked to where Lena would be buried. Amy, of course, was at her cousin's side, clasping Zara's hand, her heart, her whole being together with a force of will. But then, neither husband nor child were ready for everything that had happened, would still happen, even though they had known for months about the return of Lena's cancer.

Zara, head in a cloud of her own hair, her limbs beneath a dress of black cotton that Aunty Rose had foisted on her via Amy. Black was required funeral garb, even when the deceased was your own mother. The funeral guests had to look inside of Zara's hair cloud to see where she was. Yes, there was a pair of sad eyes.

"She was very special," an elderly woman said.

"Thank you." *She was my mother, I know.*

"She was such a good, decent soul was our Lena," added a woman that Zara had never seen before. *She was my mother!*

"She was a true revolutionary," a young man, as young as Zara, said shaking her hand feebly.

"How so?" Zara looked up stunned. Of all the things people would say at funerals, was there no limit? She knew, above any other that her mother who had, after all, belonged to her, had argued and raged but had not accomplished much from her chair, had she?

"She was my teacher," the young man said, blinking fast. "She taught me science ... standards 9 and 10 ... I didn't like all those equations and vectors, but somehow she made it seem like I could do them. But what I really remember," he went quieter yet, "was that she always asked that we think and question everything, to never take the easiest way out, even if it is convenient ... that's what she asked us to always do, I remember. She asked for something more from us," he said, patting Zara's hands gently with his own. It would be alright, the calluses on his palms, his broken nails, seemed to say. Everything would be alright.

Zara recognised the man's face instantly, years later, looking back at her from a newspaper.

A whistleblower. Dead. After his employer had constructed houses like playthings, so they collapsed onto their sleeping inhabitants during the first winter storm.

Perhaps then, a quiet revolutionary like his teacher, after all.

In the years that followed Lena's death, no one counted on the cavity that would grow inside Bart; that grew to a longing that could not be filled until the hole ate away his body and soon even his mind grew quiet and empty. Nothing could raise ire or joy in him. Not when his tea was delivered to him cold and undrinkable. Not when his favourite food was put before him or when his sister

Rose shouted into his ear, "How are you brother?" even though his hearing was fine.

Bart didn't blink when he saw his daughter graduate in the top ten of her class and enter the PhD programme ahead of schedule. All reasonable assumption was that Bart too, was making his way out of life. Slowly and feebly. When Zara listened to her father speak of betrayal one day months before his death, as he rocked on the *stoep* of the house beneath the hill with Thelonious Monk in the background, she knew he too was already gone.

30

Somewhere in the middle of one night, despite the weeks that had gone by, Zara recalled the married name the judge had given her for Marybeth after she'd married: Schuster, or no, Schusler, he had said.

A stream of people called Marybeth Schusler came up on social networking sites: one from Miami, impossibly blonde and happy, others still, who did not fit the profile. Zara began again, trying different variants of this name and surname until she had exhausted every possibility, and only when Zara returned to her desk later, after she had stared aimlessly down at Bloomfield Avenue for an hour, a cup of instant coffee in her hands, did she enter a spelling for the name she had once seen somewhere, inside a pharmacy or perhaps on a bottle of headache pills: Schucesler.

There she was. Three quarters down the page, an article listed Marybeth Schueesler, a lawyer who had lived in Toronto until her death in the late eighties.

Zara waited until the sun began to rouse Bloomfield Avenue and as soon as it was time, phoned the legal centre that Marybeth Schueesler had once worked at in Toronto.

"I never heard of this person," the young receptionist replied, in an accent Zara guessed to be Congolese. Perhaps there was someone who would be able to help her though, she said, reading off a name and number to Zara.

The old man at the other end of the line required her to repeat her name four times.

"Zara Black," he said eventually back to her, and asked that she explain herself again from the beginning. "Marybeth Schueesler, you say?"

"Did you know her? I am doing research on South Africans who left the country around the time she did," Zara said, deciding that the truth was better left unsaid.

"Marybeth Schueesler ... that name takes me back. But she died a long time ago, before I retired. In the eighties or early nineties, if I'm not wrong."

"I'm sorry to hear that."

"Well, I didn't know her well. Not outside of work. She wasn't easy to make conversation with, if you know what I mean. Kept pretty much to herself."

"But she was South African ... the woman I am looking for ..."

"I remember that she married a local doctor from around here. He died some five or maybe six years ago. It made the papers. Good sort. I don't think there was a child," he paused, "Ah, that's the lunch time bell, and Tuesday is lamb stew day. So I have to go ... I hope you understand, but I didn't know anything else about her."

"Of course ... but, Marybeth, you're certain she was South African?" Zara interrupted.

"You know I seem to recall that there was something in the papers once. Yes, it was probably in the Toronto Globe or the Daily Sun ... they came to interview her one time. We were excited because matters concerning refugees and the centre didn't always attract media, if you see my point. But then the reporter said he was writing the piece about her. Like I said, she never said much about herself, so we were surprised to learn that she was South African, yes ... that was where she had come from, South Africa, and she had done important things there."

"Is there any chance that you remember the year?"

"I can't even remember yesterday's date, but today, you're in luck. That reporter came around my fiftieth birthday, 20 March 1982. We had a cake at the centre that week, yes, they threw me a party, balloons, candles the whole nine yards," he said kindly, and then was gone.

The library that housed backdated copies of local newspapers was easy to locate, but finding a librarian who might stay with her for the duration of the conversation seemed impossible, until finally she was put through to someone who didn't have books to file or deadlines to meet.

"You would have to come here yourself; come and view the paper in our reading room ... anything that goes that far back would be on the Microfilm or if you're lucky it might be digitised, dear."

Perhaps it was the thin vein of sleep that separated the previous day from the new one, or the burden that had slipped over Zara to right a gaping wrong; and she found herself telling the librarian everything, what had happened, her father's role and who Marybeth had been. Words that she could not find with Amy or Ling came rushing out. And then somehow, incredibly, the woman agreed: she would find some time to search for the article that had been published around March 1982.

The digitised article arrived one week later in Zara's inbox.

Marybeth Harrison was not how Zara had imagined her at all. Time had done its work and there was no pale yellow sundress or heavily made up eyes or the red-mouthed smile which Zara, after all, had painted on her. Instead, there she sat in black and white, exhausted by the years, her beige stockings gathering around her ankles in thick folds.

"Was it hard going into exile, in the, was it 1960's?" the reporter had asked.

"1968."

"Right, 1968. Have you ever regretted having to leave the country of your birth?"

"Well, I am not much drawn to gratuitous emotions like regret and pity, but the choice was not mine at all ..."

"Are you still involved with South Africa? Do you still work with the ANC in exile?"

"As time passes, naturally it becomes more difficult to stay involved to the same degree ... when one lives in another country, with its own exigencies, its own timeline even ... things change. One's focus therefore must correspond. But I do try to be supportive. I do what I can. I help where I can."

"Could you tell us in more detail the reasons for your departure from South Africa?"

"I have already said it was not my choice. And there is really little else to be said on the matter. Many people had to flee, then. The State was terrorising its own citizens, persecuting people for trying to attain freedom for all."

'Were you persecuted by the National Party?"

"Many people were."

"But would you say that you were?"

"You are trying to make too fine a point of my own involvement ... many people experienced far worse than I ever did. The very act of living in a country, your own country, yet where you were required to carry a pass, live in places that were specifically allocated, with no rights to speak of. These were all acts of persecution of various degrees. Many lost children, or parents, sometimes killed before them, while others vanished, never to be seen again. But you must know all of this. Any efforts on my part are to be seen as part of a collective."

"Do you plan to return when liberation is achieved? When Nelson Mandela is set free?"

"That still seems far off, at least, in the imagination. But yes, I have always thought that that is what would happen. I have made a life here in Toronto with my husband, who is a doctor, and Seth, my son, who is still in junior school. Life is more complicated and the decision isn't mine alone. But certainly ... certainly, I dream of nothing else."

*

Zara had walked past the café many times before, and yet she had never noticed it, tucked between a speciality paper store that sold every conceivable shade, texture and pattern of paper, and an organic food market that sold fruits from around the planet.

She found a seat in the corner, her back facing the large white tiles that recalled a Parisian subway or a kitchen in a hospital, and then she waited. Fifteen minutes later, when she began to hope that perhaps he would not show up after all, Seth Schueesler, hair carefully ruffled and a t-shirt hanging loosely beneath a denim jacket, entered the café. He barely differed from the picture she had seen of him online; a rising movie maker, he was slightly older than her, but youthful, nonetheless.

Zara signalled.

"Zara? I'm Seth," he said, offering her his hand. "That was an interesting call I got from you," he said, smiling and finding a place for his bag, his book-sized laptop, his phone and an iPod, and sat across from her.

"Thank you for meeting me. I know it must seem strange to receive a call out of the blue like this, but there was something I hoped we could speak about."

"Yeah? Can I get you a coffee? I'll take a cappuccino, no sugar," he said, turning to speak to the waiter. "So what's this all about? You have me intrigued; you said you were doing research about my mom, and on South Africa, right?"

"Seth, I didn't quite tell you everything on the phone, because I think what I have to say to you is best said in person ... I know who your mother was, and it seems I now also know the reasons why she left South Africa."

"Who did you say you were again?" he said, examining her.

"I recently learned that my father may have had something to do with your mother's departure."

"Zara, what did you say your last name was?" His voice had turned interrogative.

"Black. I'm Zara Black and your mother knew my father, Bart Black."

His eyes slid across her face and to the cappuccino that had been delivered before him.

"I have heard of your father," he said.

"Have you?" Zara studied him in turn. "I know this must be difficult for you ... it has been nothing but awful since I first found out what my father is said to have done, from a mutual friend of theirs, James Ndlovu. I met with him here in New York a few days back and he told me everything. I don't know what you know ..."

"Perhaps it would be best if you told me what you know," he said, his voice terse, his eyes drifting over to the wide glass doors to watch the young couple standing squarely in the window frame, a lime green umbrella opened above them that held off the sun.

Zara told him everything: the story sealing them into a world and place far removed, fifty years before, as Zara studied his profile, his aviator sunglasses holding back brown hair. She faltered, stopped for a minute, began again and only when she had told the story as it had been told to her by the judge, did Zara go silent.

"And what exactly do you want from me?" His face flashed.

"I just thought ... perhaps we could speak about it. What my father did. How your mother survived those years away from home ... perhaps you would allow me to ask if you have heard all of this before. I'm not really sure: To make things right, if that is at all possible?" she said, and felt ashamed.

"That's impossible," he said, looking at her directly. "You cannot *make right* when my mother is long dead. Do you know that she never went back? Not even once? Do you know that she died in Toronto, without ever having gone back?"

"Yes."

"Whatever you had in mind, well I'm sorry to be the one to tell you, but it's too late."

She followed his eyes to the street; the women dressed in heels or pumps, in miniskirts, pants and dresses that dragged along the pavement, men in suits or shorts or oversized jeans on a road that seemed to be every city and yet no place in particular. From the road, she saw strangers return their gaze, maybe wondering at this pair, seemingly locked in an endless moment of conflict. Certainly, none could have imagined them to be strangers connected by the thinnest arc of history.

"Look," he began, after a long time had passed, "you have to understand that you cannot just show up and tell me these things, and then what? Expect some sort of conversation? Reconciliation? Is that what you want from me, on behalf of your father? You've caught me by surprise ... my mother died many years ago, and I haven't thought about this stuff for a very long time. I'm not sure this meeting was a good idea ..."

"I just thought perhaps you could tell me what you knew ... whether you had heard this version of events, could confirm the details so that I could understand why my father acted the way he did ... but I suppose that was unfair."

"You make it sound as if your father did this only one time? Are you sure about that?" he demanded, angrily.

Zara hesitated: "I am not sure of anything anymore. But I would hope ..."

"My mother often spoke about *Askaris* ... informants ... she had no sympathy for them ... she spoke about it from first-hand knowledge!" He exhaled loudly, walked to the bathroom and returned a few minutes later, calmer.

"I know some of this story," he began. "I knew that my mom had been betrayed by someone very close to her. I didn't know about the judge's role in all of this. I didn't know as much as you've just told me. But I remember your father's name because after she died,

I had to pack up her things. She had an old shoe box at the top of her wardrobe. I had never seen this box before. It had little mementos, not much, but things which must have been important to her: pictures of her when she was a child, photos of family and friends, some birthday cards, ones that I'd made, and a few letters. Among these, I found a letter from Bart Black; a name I have not forgotten. It was no more than half a page. He wrote, and I remember it clearly, that he wasn't asking for her forgiveness, he had no right to that, but he said he wanted her to know that he had lived with his shame every day. I wondered then if he had been the one that betrayed her. I don't know if she ever wrote back."

Zara felt her resolve give way entirely. She let the tears run down her face as Seth spoke.

"There was always something with my mother, some melancholy that I couldn't understand, and that she would never name. I mean, yeah, she made a life for us. She had my dad, and they were happy ... as happy as any couple, I guess. But there was always something," he grabbed a fistful of air. "I figured it was home, a longing which she couldn't quite share with us, or family ... not that they wanted anything to do with her until almost the very end, no, she had been the rebel, the traitor who had turned her back on her people ... at least, that was how *they* saw it," he said. "Something was always missing." He stopped to take a sip of his cold coffee and cleared his voice. "I know now, it wasn't as simple as a longing for home. It was the memories of what had happened, everything that forced her away, everything that she had to leave behind. She died that way."

31

September passed in a haze.

The campus bus was late again. It was eight thirty five in the morning and Zara's skin had turned a sticky bronze sheen as she perspired beneath the sun- yellow awning of Ortez and Sons.

"'Scuse the delay, honey," the bus driver managed out of breath, when Zara climbed aboard the bus ten minutes after its scheduled arrival. "I know everyone's got a beef with me this morning," the woman continued hurriedly, a sprinkling of sweat covering her face as she apologised and motioned to the front row passengers who exhibited none of their usual cool stares, but were clearly annoyed as they waited to be delivered to their air-conditioned offices. Zara took her place beside the driver, leaning against the railing.

"Too hot, that's what it is: people don't like it too hot or too cold. That's human nature, never happy with one thing or the other. And this," she said, shooting an accusatory glance at the sky, "we call it Indian Summer – hot but it's already late September ..." the driver continued, speaking to herself as she pulled up sharply at a stop sign.

"You alright Merle? You seem in a rush today," Zara said, regaining her balance and steadying herself against a pole.

"I'm sorry honey, got an interview in thirty minutes, can't be late," she said, focussing on the road ahead of her.

"Are you leaving us?" Zara asked, the tone of sadness genuine. She looked forward to Merle's stories about her son and the conversations they shared on mornings when Zara took the bus to work.

"Maybe ... maybe. If I get a job on campus, up at the post office. It's for my boy," she continued, and Zara automatically looked at the picture on the dashboard where her son still smiled back at his mother. "No tuition costs for the family of university employees, be one more thing off my plate ..."

"Well, I'll definitely miss you Merle. Half the reason I take the bus is to catch up with you, but I *really* hope you get it," Zara said.

"Yeah? Well that's nice of you. That's real nice of you to say," she said, relaxing for a minute. "Keep you posted," she called out, as she let Zara off at the Humanities building and prepared to speed away, the front row passengers muttering openly.

When she reached her desk, Zara placed the call that she had not stopped thinking about for days. The phone was answered quickly by a young woman. His daughter, Zara would later learn.

"The judge is not taking any calls. Who? Zara Black. Oh. Oh, yes I see." She was not asked to wait, but heard efficient footsteps retreating, followed by voices in the background.

The judge came to the phone a minute later.

"Zara? Is it you?"

"Hello, Judge Ndlovu. How are you? Have I disturbed you? I could call back if you prefer," she asked, hesitantly.

"No, you have saved me from myself, I can't seem to find my book ... I was sure it was here," he said, drifting off. "No, let us speak. I am fine ... good ... yes, thank you."

"Really?"

"Under the circumstances."

"I saw a recording of the press conference. You've retired?"

"It will give me time to spend with your Aunty Violet. You know she has been complaining for thirty years that she hasn't seen me. And now she complains that I am everywhere: in her kitchen, in her bathroom, in her lounge. Anyway, you should see my roses. The gardener has been regularly decapitating them, so I have all the time in the world now to watch over them," he said, with a thin note of assurance.

"And you're sure about all of this?"

He cleared his voice, and she heard a door slide gently closed.

"Well Zara, you know, really I was left with no choice. All I had left to say was that, yes, I am guilty for that which I stand accused. After all these years I could not bring Marybeth into it. We are at an interregnum now, Zara. We will have to see what happens next, who comes to power and how. It makes sense that I step out of the way ... for the sake of the judiciary, if nothing and no one else," he spoke slowly and carefully.

"You didn't mention my father's name either."

"There isn't much sense dragging him into it now. It was such a long time ago ..."

"I thought that you had every right ..."

"What is the point of this finger pointing now when Bart is dead and cannot defend himself, and the next thing, well, they will be calling you ... and this is not your fight ..."

"I'm not sure ..." Zara began, but the judge interrupted her.

"I have been thinking. I should have said all of this to you when we met. Zara," he dropped his voice, "... maybe I threw the first punch with Bart, as they say. But if he had walked away from me and Marybeth, left it at that, perhaps I would have apologised and perhaps in time he would have forgiven me. For everything. You see, I missed Bart's friendship over the years. He never could bring himself to face me. Still, Zara, despite all I have said ... I want to ask you, maybe you know: why? He handed us over to the enemy! Was this not a punishment too great for the crime? Was it a moment of madness? An aberration? Do you know, Zara? Because I don't understand ..."

"I was hoping you could tell me," she said, very softly. After a moment had passed, the judge still silent at the other end, she continued: "Judge, do you know if there was another time that he spoke to the police, or was it just the once?"

"That is what I don't know, Zara. I hope ... I imagine the man that I once knew would never have done that to us, his friends."

"All I can reason is that my father had weaknesses, passions and I guess cruelty too, which at least that once, got the better of him."

"No matter, then, no matter. I must still take responsibility for the people who were harmed. The day before the press conference, and this is what pressed me to make up my mind ... someone called me, Zara. She said she believed that my betrayal had led to the arrest of her father. He was picked up days after I was – but he was a true hero. He refused to speak ... and died weeks later in police custody." His voice faded. "I think ... no matter why this information has been released, there can be no escaping it – it is my responsibility and I will face that child, after all, her father was killed because of my actions."

The line went so quiet Zara thought that she had lost him, but the distant suburban sounds, a door opening and the clicking of heels, indicated that he was still on the other end.

Finally Zara came to the reason for her call: "Is it wrong to admit that I wish he had been amongst the brave who stood for days and weeks of torture, refusing to give in rather than being the traitor? Well, I do. He betrayed. That is the word. He never atoned. So no, whether I choose this or not, apparently, it is mine. And I am sorry for what my father did to you."

"Thank you Zara." She heard shuffling, a long pause, and then the line went dead.

32

"Zee, do something, please. Have a press conference or at least speak to this journalist friend I told you about. All this obfuscation and sleight of hand does no one any good. Before you come back, you will need to face this, so you can face yourself. Anyway, they had no right releasing names when people are dead and cannot defend themselves." Amy's words reverberated across the line when Zara told her about the conversation with the judge.

"I'm not sure Amy. The information would probably have been released one day anyway ... isn't it the country's right to know this information?"

"Theoretically perhaps ... but practically, I have my questions about it all. What loaded terms: betrayal, forgiveness, reconciliation. I'm tired of it all. And the way it was done. This was a warning shot and not at all about justice. Your father just got caught up in a messy business. So I have my doubts," replied Amy.

But for once her cousin's goodness felt out of place, too contrived for the stuff that Zara needed.

"Amy, I don't want more publicity, I want less. I want none at all. I want to get on with my life ..."

That her life had begun to move in new directions, Zara did not mention to Amy. Jan, the head of the history department, a woman who Zara only saw at monthly meetings and had barely spoken with, had arrived unannounced in Zara's office early one morning. Rapping an officious tap-tap on the door, she'd entered, hovered momentarily, and noticed judiciously that Ling's desk seemed unused.

"Oh, she'll be in later today," Zara had answered a little too defensively. Zara had been away from her office for a few days after she'd heard the news about her father. She had told Jan that she needed some time to sort out a family matter, though Zara doubted this was reason enough. If she had learned anything it was that Americans did not admit to illness and crisis, and certainly never took holidays for much longer than a week if they wanted to be seen as productive. With Jan's unexpected appearance, Zara realised she may have overstepped her mark.

"I wanted to have a word with you," the lithe yoga master had said, as she positioned herself on the corner of Ling's desk.

"Yes, of course," Zara had prepared for a dressing down.

"How's your time here been?" she'd asked instead, with a professional smile. "Good? Good," Jan had forged ahead without waiting for a reply. "Actually, I'm here because I wanted to tell you about a post that's opening up in a couple of months," she had continued, as lissom arms and long ringed fingers opened and arced and spoke a language of their own.

"Oh ... I ... that's interesting," Zara had been surprised.

"Yes, well, actually it's been one headache after another. We've lost two lecturers this semester alone. Damned South Hall keeps poaching my staff," Jan had continued, as her fingers performed an arabesque in the direction of the college on the other side of town. "Point is, I will need someone who could hit the ground running, so to speak. Of course, the said person would have to apply through all the appropriate channels, go through the university panel and so on, obviously have the right qualifications ... like you," she'd said, as her arms came to a rest and she looked at Zara closely. "I'd like you to apply."

"Really? I didn't ... I have a few months left on my fellowship," Zara had said, stunned that she had even been noticed in those often quiet rooms.

"Hard work impresses me. And I was very interested in your Timbuktu paper that you delivered last month. And more interested in a paper you delivered when you just arrived, was it: *South Africa and racial reconciliation at the end of the 20th century?* America is facing one of its most interesting times," Jan had pressed on as her hand swept across the newspaper that Zara had left on Ling's desk that morning – the word HISTORY had been printed in large font above a picture of the country's Democrat presidential candidate staring into a jubilant crowd. "There is an opportunity for a fresh debate on race, within its historical context, of course. We should talk it all up – Jim Crow, black pride to post-racism," she'd said, pushing herself nimbly onto Ling's desk. "And who could think of a more appropriate time? I'm looking for someone to champion a project for me, and South Africa was such an example of reconciliation ..."

"Well, we felt that we'd achieved a great deal in a short time. And we did, we made many advances. On the other hand, I think we're learning more and more that reconciliation is a process that will take time and genuine effort ..." Zara had replied, looking away cautiously.

But the dean did not seem to have heard Zara, "What needs to be asked is: can we transcend not as individuals but as a country? Because that is the real challenge: is America really ready to elect a member of a minority, a black man, as president? Think about it, this could be a great opportunity for everyone. Let me know," she'd said finally, turned and left.

*

When Ling arrived back from her two week vacation in California she was glowing and even slimmer than before.

"Zara, I was worried ... are you alright?"

"I'm fine Ling, really, thanks for all the calls and emails. I'm sorry I didn't respond, but I needed to take care of some things."

"In other words, none of my business? Look, I should have stuck around to check if you were ok. But you didn't answer my calls – not mine nor Michael's. So I went on holiday instead. Guess that makes me a bit of a shit, huh?"

"Of course not."

'Ok, well then, I am listening."

Zara told Ling about her father and about her decision to come and study in the United States.

"That's heavy," Ling replied, after listening quietly. "Would it make you feel any better if I told you that my family left China under something of a cloud? My Dad used to be an important member of the government ... but you know, things turned bad, he fell out with his seniors and it became impossible for us to stay. We were lucky to all get out together."

"Could you ever go back?"

'I don't know Zara ... it's funny, but my dad doesn't let a day go by without speaking about *when* we go back; never if, only when."

"So we are both exiles then?"

"No, we are the children of men who made choices which have fallen on us."

That evening Zara took her time walking back to her place on Bloomfield Avenue. She greeted Mr Ortez who was closing up his shop. They waved at each other, strangers or friends? Perhaps a little of each.

Then she went back to her room, ready to finish with her father.

*

What must Bart and Marybeth's shouting have sounded like beyond those porous walls to the neighbours?

"What do you want from me?"

"We have nothing in common!"

"Then leave ..."

"Fine, in fact I'd be happy to! God, what a sissy, always moaning about your father did this, your father did that. Your back is crooked because you're carrying a dead old man on it ..."

"Marybeth, just go ... take your bags now and leave. At least life will be halfway peaceful without having to listen to you rage against everything ..."

"While you sit and let the rest of us do your dirty work! You think being a lawyer who dispenses advice is enough? We need you out there every day. Fighting, standing up ... not this ... this passive remote resistance. Oh you make me sick!"

"Well then why are you still standing here? Go ... go ... I don't want to see you ..."

"Really? Well, funny you should say that. Because James loves looking at me ... oh, and I've been fucking him all along. Can you believe every time you bored me, I closed my eyes and thought about him?"

Is this the way it finally played out: after all the years, a pitiful soap opera? Zara cannot imagine any other way for something like this to be said.

"What? What did you say?"

That would have been the moment for Marybeth to have turned her back, shocked at her own words.

"What did you say about you and James?" Bart would have walked behind her.

"Nothing ..." but of course by then it would have been too late. He would have thrown her out, not physically of course, because Zara knew that Bart had believed that women were to be given as much, if not more, respect than men.

The rest she could not imagine. Did Bart go then and there to report a meeting he knew would take place and be illegal? Zara tried to imagine step for step, Bart walking towards the old police station down in the city. The one that Zara had driven past as a child and had always thought of as a place that was not meant for her, her family, her people. It was a police station that serviced other people's concerns: barking dogs, cats stuck up trees, suburban disturbances of all sorts. For her, and the people she knew, it was the dream catcher that caught their hopes for freedom and hid them away behind red brick walls.

And then? When he arrived, did he walk inside that place that was not theirs, and lay a complaint? Bart who did not usually know how to confront people, did he then stand before a policeman, who must have assessed him quickly and decided here was an enemy?

"She is there waiting at home." Is this what he said?

There was another possibility that Zara could only acknowledge as she let the day go and allowed sleep to wander over her – what if her father had been an informant all along? What if he had been feeding the security police information for all those years that he and Marybeth had lived together? Or had he become friends with James, and Marybeth's lover, all so that he could spy on them and the movement? It was not impossible; how many stories had been revealed after the fall of apartheid about family members, and close friends who had done exactly this? The idea kept her sleepless.

No, she couldn't fathom it at all. The answers were buried along with her father, mother and Marybeth Harrison. The past was mostly sewn up. Only its rotten fingers were left dangling for the world to gawk at.

33

It was late in the day, the light turning copper. Zara was noticing just this as she hastened to a meeting that had been called at the last minute, when a familiar voice called her name from behind. It was her friend the erstwhile bus driver, rushing to catch up with her, a huge and heavy bag slung over her shoulder.

"Merle, where have you been? It's been weeks," said Zara warmly, turning and waiting. Since Merle had changed jobs, Zara missed their regular conversations.

"Yeah, I looked for you – heard you were off sick. You alright?"

"I'm good now. You?"

"Well, I got that job up in the post office and I've been real busy. See I'm a postman," she said, and chuckled, indicating the bag laden with letters and university circulars.

"So you are. How's your son?" Zara asked, recalling the image of the smiling teen.

"Oh, he's just great," Merle's face broke into that characteristic expression of joy, and her coil of braids nodded in agreement. "He's just great."

"And how are things going with his studies?"

"Well, we changed plan a bit. See, even with the university remittance this job isn't quite enough for everything he's gonna need. No way, no, a scholar of engineering needs books, equipment, and a room, and food and clothes ... oh my, the list is just as long as my arm," Merle continued, offering her arm as proof. "So he's joining the army," she said, shifting from one foot to the other.

"Oh. They'll pay for his studies?" Zara asked, digging her hands into her pockets, her face mirroring Merle's frown.

"They'll pay for schooling, give him a real career, and the discipline will do him good too," Merle's voice began to fade, but her feet continued shifting as if the ground were heating up where she stood. "He'll be alright. I just know he will."

"Well, then, that's what matters," Zara agreed.

"And you know when the new president is elected, well, he's gonna end the war. Everything will be fine."

"Yes, I hope so. But we should make a time to chat properly ... I have a meeting to get to, but come look me up in Humanities. We'll grab a cup of coffee, alright?" Zara said, with strict sincerity and began to walk away, all the while watching Merle.

"That sounds real nice, honey. Yep, I gotta rush now too, I'll come find you ..." she said, and started walking backwards, before she spun on her heels and vanished into the crowd of students.

*

The grand clock that stood in Jan's office, had just turned six, when Zara made her way into the room. Books lined the wall on one side, and the other was occupied by framed pictures. It was here that Zara occupied herself as the dean called out a hasty hello, ushering Zara in as she continued the telephone conversation she was having. The pictures on the wall were the who's who of world leaders, businessmen, politicians.

"I used to teach at Baler," Jan began, once her conversation had ended. "I met all of them back in those days, before I moved here to be close to my mother ... cancer," she said plainly, without slowing her pace, or glancing up from what she was doing, before she changed the subject. "What I want to know is if you've thought about our conversation?" Jan jumped right in, so that Zara had to leave off looking at the pictures and make her way towards the empty chair on the opposite side of her desk.

"I thought I had two months before applications closed?"

"Yes, but that was the president of the university with whom I was just speaking. She has given the go ahead for us to start my new project as soon as possible," Jan said, her chin poised as she searched for a pen beneath sheets of paper and open books. "These are historic times Zara, historic! The presidential election that few thought we would see in our lifetime is around the corner," the dean said, and met Zara's eyes as she settled for the moment. "So you see this project has taken on some urgency and normally the process of funding would take years, but in this instance, well, I have the whole university board and president urging me to get started." Jan moved delicate, toned arms about with great efficiency and a hint of drama. She asked pointedly: "Are you in or out?"

"I didn't expect you to ask me here today with any sort of deadline," Zara said, bothered that she was unprepared. She had not yet made up her mind whether she would apply for the position.

"Yes, of course. Of course," the dean continued, a note of annoyance now straining her voice. "You would still have to apply, but like I've said before, I will need someone to get the project off the ground quickly. And you're a likely candidate. Perhaps even the favourite at this point. So I must insist that you think about it and let me know in the coming weeks."

"Ok, I will think about it," Zara said, and rose to leave.

*

Perhaps Zara would have wandered on in that self-styled purgatory for years. Believing she had found some resolution with her past, despite the fact that she felt herself to be breathing very slowly. She had begun avoiding Jan and the question of why she had not yet applied for the available position at Berwick University; she sidestepped Amy's insistence that she should consider returning home to sort matters out for herself, all the while wondering whether Michael would answer his phone if she finally called him.

She might have gone on like that, had the chaos of the past year not fallen away in the ensuing bedlam.

The news came in shards of information via the telephone, email and text messages from Amy: Aunty Rose had been robbed while on her weekly trip to the store. She was in hospital, seriously injured. And in shock, unable, or perhaps unwilling, to speak.

Aunty Rose had observed the same habit for some forty years. Every Wednesday afternoon, failing illness or Cape Town's driving rain that could find you at any angle, Aunty Rose dressed in one of her good skirts, a twin cardigan set, stockings, and a sturdy pair of leather loafers. She drew a line of lipstick across her lips and two small moons of blush on either cheek. Sometime in the last two decades she had dispensed with the gloves and hat. Then she went shopping. This, despite the fact that Amy delivered her groceries to her and that she'd been asking her mother to wait until she could take her shopping on Saturday afternoons. The area had become too dangerous. Yes, there were still neighbours who she knew to greet and chat with, who observed her out of concern and others who checked that her lights had been switched on or off. But there were also youths roaming the streets high on drugs, looking for an open window or a kind smile, and gangsters just waiting to pounce on an old lady. Still, the weekly shop was a small concession with which Amy could live, and a freedom that Aunty Rose could not live without.

Had Amy known that she wore a diamond ring to visit the local store, the police had asked? But of course she had not. She would have discouraged it naturally, but even then, her mother was, despite all the dangers and her age, still a free agent.

"Why would she wear the ring to go shopping, Zee?" Amy had asked in the days that followed, her voice taut with hurt or guilt or anger or all of these together. "It makes no sense."

She had already left the grocery store, a slab of Swiss chocolate in her handbag alongside a packet of jelly sweets. The police determined that she had been walking or perhaps standing on the pavement, ready to cross the road. Had she swerved for the young mother pushing the pram? Or perhaps, and more likely, she had been pushed. A witness inside the pharmacy had only seen her when she was already lying at the side of the road, her hands covering her head as the young woman (who could say if there had been a baby in the pram at all) pulled off the ring, checked Aunty Rose's handbag, taking her purse and leaving everything else. By the time the security guard who was posted inside the pharmacy had been called, Aunty Rose was lying face down in the street, a line of blood woven into her hair.

"Can she speak?" Zara asked, her voice moving in uncertain arcs.

"She nods. She cries a lot. You know, aside from my father's funeral, I don't recall ever seeing her cry."

"The ring was her father's gift to her."

Each evening the telephone conversations endured as Aunty Rose remained in hospital, the blow to her head healing slowly, while the broken hip would take months of recovery. Conscious, but never speaking a word.

34

"You know, Miss, my name is not actually Ortez," the man standing before Zara spoke again, smiled and tilted his head. "I am Vince Alvarez."

It was early in the morning. Sleep was coming slowly to Zara these days and when it did come, it washed over her gently, gurgling in her ears instead of the total submersion and paralysis which she longed for. Instead, she had become attuned to waking up at three a.m, so that she could answer Amy's calls which had come almost every night for the past two weeks. Amy was taking an extended leave of absence and she called Zara each morning on reaching the hospital in which Aunty Rose was recuperating. With nothing to do and uncertain of how to be a visitor in any hospital, she walked to her car while the doctors were making their rounds, and placed a call to Zara.

"How's your mom?"

"Weak. Some of the wounds have healed, but she is simply not recovering. They did an MRI and can't see any damage ... she recognises me, but doesn't speak."

"It may take time ..."

"Zee, I've seen this before: an aged person has a fall, and after ... afterwards there is simply no will to recover ... and then it wasn't a fall, but an attack ..."

Zara stood before Mr Ortez – or rather Mr Alvarez. "Oh ... oh," Zara stammered, the words drifting through the cool morning air, into her ear, via myriad passageways and tubes and pumping blood vessels, every one of which she could feel at that moment. "Alvarez? I'm sorry I just assumed because of the sign," Zara felt her cheeks heating as she pointed to the evidence, *Ortez and Sons, Quality Tobacco Merchants since 1950.*

"Yes, the sign. Actually, the store, it is part of a franchise operation. There are two hundred and fifty two stores just like this one all over the country. I've worked here now for ... let me see ... twelve years next March," he said, and used his fingers to check. "And my name is Alvarez," he said, and smiled again, apologetically, as if the mistake were his own.

"Well, I'm Zara and I am pleased to finally meet you," Zara said, and offered him her hand. "I suppose I'll see you tomorrow then, Mr Alvarez," Zara said, reassuring both of them, before walking off, shaking her head at her error.

When Zara reached her office, Ling was already at her desk, fingers tapping earnestly at the white and silver ergonomically designed keyboard that she carried with her to work. Ling stirred at the sound of the door being pushed open, but smiled on seeing Zara.

"You alright?"

"I'm fine. Where is the emergency and why are you here at eight a.m.?" Zara asked, assessing Ling's desk. Books were piled high in a box that stood on the desk.

"Zara. I'll be leaving soon," Ling began in a calm voice.

"What do you mean?" Zara's head shot up as she descended into her chair.

"Well, it appears my fling with academia," Ling said, and threw her arms dramatically around the room, "has expired."

"I thought your father supported your studies ..."

"Apparently his support, and may I also just say his wallet, has a limit. I'm being sent to Shanghai. He has been speaking with people back home, people in government and the Party, and he thinks it's time for us to try and return. He wants me to go ahead and check it out, see whether it's viable to set up a business there ... whether *he* could return."

"Just like that?" Zara was stunned.

"Yep. He thinks I'm wasting my time here and that my duty, as his daughter, is to go ahead and see how his return will be perceived."

"But your parents could go without you, Ling, and you could refuse!"

"Zara, my family doesn't work that way, and I need to do this for him. My Dad's spent nearly twenty years dreaming about going home. He hasn't seen his parents, has no idea how the country, the cities have changed ... all he knows is what he hears from others and sees on television! And now that there has been an opening in relations, he feels that he ... we ... should take it. I have to do this."

Zara sat back. The patterns of her life would just not hold still and she was beginning to believe that she should not expect, from one day to the next, the world to stay the same.

"This place feels bare already," Zara said, miserably.

"I know. Anyway, how about some breakfast? I've been here since seven thirty and I'm starving!" Ling said, in fake cheeriness, so they rose and walked together to the cafeteria for the final time.

35

The city and the country had descended into presidential fervour. The election would be held soon. From what Zara could tell, the world itself had come a little undone in all the excitement; the election playing out as only an American one ever could: on every channel, in every conversation, on every pair of lips.

Ling's apartment was warm and festive for the fundraising party. Her final, before departing for Shanghai.

Six-foot cardboard cut-outs of the nation's potential president beamed as guests and contributors took their pictures beside it, teeth displayed and fingers poised in peace signs. Escaped balloons swayed with the chandelier, while people with cocktails milled and chatted beneath.

Zara was standing at Pedro's side, handing him beakers and bottles, an attentive assistant in this very important operation.

"Now, you pour very, very slowly," Pedro was saying gently as he slid a layer of cream onto a liqueur base, "because you really don't want it to mix ... see?" he said victorious, and handed Zara the drink. She was standing with Gianna, a bare shoulder pressed to the wall.

"Only problem is America will start speaking on top of the voice again," Gianna was saying, her bony fingers pushing her black spectacles hard onto her face. This got Pedro rolling his eyes at Zara. "At least the last few years Americans stopped being so noisy, you felt a bit embarrassed ... your President left something to be desired and this made you quiet for a while, no?" Gianna taunted Luke unashamedly.

"Not tonight Gianna, seriously ..." replied Luke.

"And then we will have to hear on and on how your country is the greatest country in the world. That this is only possible in America. Don't you ever think, maybe, this is something you mustn't say to the rest of the world? That maybe this is what upsets us? Don't you think Zara," Gianna continued, throwing Zara's name into the air like an arrow.

But now, before she could be included any further, Zara felt a tapping on her shoulder.

"How are you, Michael?" Zara asked, turning around.

"Good ... I am good. You?" He looked around the room, his expression never wavering.

"Fine, thank you. I'm fine."

"What have you been up to since I last saw you?" he asked, so that Zara spotted an almost imperceptible ache cross his face.

"Michael, I should tell you ... I had a terrible time. Family illness, betrayal, lies ... you know ... the usual," she said, "But I am sorry that I didn't return your calls ..."

"Sure. Of course, I understand. Listen, I see someone I haven't seen in a while ... catch up later, alright?" He was off across the room, leaving Zara standing alone and feeling slighted.

She spent the evening hanging around Pedro, trying to avoid the small talk, all the while hoping that Michael might at least speak to her. When she found him standing silently beside her, she turned to face him: "Michael, I liked you, I really did. I had things to sort out ... matters which, in all honesty, felt like they might overtake me at times. I hope you understand," Zara said, and began to move away.

"This election is exciting, really exciting, right? Although ..." replied Michael, before Zara had turned entirely away.

"Yes?"

"I dunno – what do you do when someone you really like, who you somehow – rarely as it happens – think you may have had something with, vanishes ..." He looked at her fully, plaintively.

"I know ... I am sorry ..."

"C'mon ..." he said, gently guiding her to the balcony.

Standing outside on the narrow walkway, an ashtray piled high with cigarette butts and dust that had grown into pot plants and chairs, Zara spoke without hesitation and only stopped once she had unloaded it all: her Aunty Rose, and what she had learned about her father.

"You know," Michael began once Zara had ended. "We're not responsible for the messes our parents make."

"You see, that's what I'm not sure about. I inherited the house that my father inherited in turn from his father ... do I also inherit some of the blame? I could never understand why my father would never live in that house until we had no choice. Well, I get it now: because if he accepted the house he was also accepting his father's betrayal of his own mother, and a piece of his crime. Take the benefit but not the blame? That's too simple."

"Yeah well, happens everywhere. Look around you. Ever heard anyone say my great granddaddy the warmonger or the slave owner? Course not, but you do hear about inherited wealth," Michael said.

"Then again, you can't drag the past around with you ... you have to ..."

"Move on ... yes ... yes, I've heard that one before. But what does that neat line mean, exactly?"

"I was going to say cut it loose. Sure, it happened. If you feel partly responsible, ok, act on it. And then? Well, either you cut it loose or you carry it with you."

By the time Zara left Ling's place at midnight, they had hugged like friends who had known each other for years, rather than the months it had been. Ling would leave for Shanghai in days to come.

"So, you know, I am fantastic at avoiding work, right? And I got your number ..."

"I swear to attend to every email and answer every call ..."

"So, just for interest's sake, are you guys an item now?" Ling asked, and indicated Michael with a flick of her mascara-heavy eyes.

"We are having coffee in the week ... I will let you know once I know," Zara smiled.

"Courting, then? Nice ... don't let it fall apart again, ok?"

"Have a safe flight, Ling. And email me once you arrive, alright?" Zara said, holding Ling tightly, before she walked quickly out of the door.

36

And then it was winter, cold and remorseless.

The office was quiet without Ling who was a world away, trying to adapt to her new life. For Zara, a paper that was due on Timbuktu kept her busy.

She met Michael for coffee and then for dinner later that week in the small Ethiopian restaurant. Two days later she caught the early train to the City so that she could meet Michael in a café that seemed to get everything right: strains of a kora in the background, light muted enough so that she could still see every expression that crossed Michael's face and the slant of his head. He had remembered everything she had told him, and he listened without distraction. They found themselves meeting up in a book store during the middle of a Sunday afternoon, paging through second hand books, twisting them over in their hands and trying out chapters on each other:

"Here: 'If I'd been black that would at least have given the information I was from Africa. Even at a three-hundred-year remove, a black American. But nobody could see me, there, for what I am back where I come from. Nobody in Paris ...'"

"Coetzee," Michael guessed.

"Gordimer ..."

Zara found herself telling Michael everything about her family and her father, raising the shame, and somehow, she felt lighter.

'When I met Seth Schueesler ... I could see that he was angry with me ... that I was the child of the person who had caused his mother so much pain ... the pain of dislocation or distance or alienation, or worse, betrayal in addition to all of that. He didn't blame my father, in that moment, but me."

"You made yourself responsible, you stood in your father's place; I think that was what you meant to do. Anyway, you should call him up now that he has had time to think through things. Try him again, he was shocked ... still, however it turns out with him, you did the right thing."

"What if it wasn't just that once that he betrayed them, Michael? What then?"

By the time two weeks had passed, Zara realised that not a day had gone by without a conversation, meeting or message between her and Michael; and she found that she did not want it any other way.

In that other world, Aunty Rose's illness endured. She was still in hospital, her recovery slow. One after the other friends, cousins and her long lost sister had been to visit, from England, from Australia and from the other side of the city. For Amy, the visitors represented the surest omen yet that her mother would not recover. All the arrivals were accompanied by sombre moods and all the departures blessed with tears and complaints against the country, crime, the world itself. Aunty Rose would search each face, only for a moment, before shutting her eyes.

Amy reported all of this all through a cloud of exhaustion.

"Everyone's been to visit. Is there something I need to know? The sister that she has not seen in a decade pitched up – she called me from the airport!"

But after a while, even the uninvited visitors dried up. So that Amy was left alone again. And when she quit her job to watch over her mother day and night, Zara objected.

"Amy you love your work," Zara protested.

"Well ... this is more important."

"Of course, but you need to hold onto something Amy. Medicine has always been your grounding ..."

"Really? Was it ever that? Actually, it's been pretty complicated of late, Zee."

"Amy, it's what you know ..."

"I could learn something else, surely ..."

"Like what? Needlepoint? No ... you were born for this, it's your calling, your duty ..." Zara should have known how ultimately unkind those words were for one who had always met responsibility at the door. Zara should have known that Amy, who had never turned her back on anything or anyone, knew precisely what she was walking away from.

"Did you say duty?" the words came angled out of Amy.

"What does that mean, Amy?"

"Oh Zee, you have buried yourself a world away!" Amy's fury came on suddenly. The months, and possibly even years, of rage against her cousin had finally erupted over the stress of everything else. "All of this – this whole expedition to the USA, has been an elaborate passage of escape!"

"If this is about duty Amy, then I have performed it. I apologised to Judge Ndlovu," Zara said, stunned.

"Really, Zee? And that settles it? There were more lives ruined than just yours and his ..."

"I have thought of nothing else ..."

"Really, nothing else? I think you have thought greatly about your own discomfort. The apology was as much about creating distance between you and your father as it is was about assuaging anyone else's pain."

"Amy, that's an awful thing to say. Anyway, what should I do? Stick up for the guy who betrayed his friends in the worst possible way, because he is my father?"

"Your father was betrayed too, Zara, however slight it may seem to you. Anyway, if not you, then who precisely? He was a good man in extraordinary circumstances."

"I cannot believe I am hearing this from you, of all people, Amy! What should I tell Judge Ndlovu? That he was wrong? And shall I tell Seth that his heartbroken mother was wrong for what she did to my father?"

"They were!"

"It's not the same, Amy, a personal betrayal versus a betrayal of an idea, a people ... he never atoned! And what if this wasn't a once-off occurrence, what if he was a monster? A serial betrayer?"

"He was no monster! Where in this morally ideal universe of yours does humanity feature, Zara? What was Bart Black's life, if not atonement? He gave up law, he lived with the shame of what he had done – that was clear enough to anyone who knew him. He asked in a million ways for clemency. You just don't see it."

"He betrayed his friends ..."

"Yes Zee ... yes, even decent people betrayed! The country was not, contrary to all expectation, split into villains and heroes.

Sometimes ordinary people, good people, fucked up, Zee. What if your father made a mistake? A horrible, regrettable mistake that would follow him for the rest of his life? This great struggle of ours – my God, what a legacy it has left us: we must not see anyone but the victor, the hero, the winning narrative. No, we have painted over the past as it was, and replaced it with something which is pleasing to the eye. A one dimensional story!"

"So what would you have me do? Come home, carry the shame around for him? Is that my duty Amy?"

"Come home or don't. But see him for what he was. A flawed man. Not an enemy of the people." She went quiet. But Zara could still hear her short breaths, sense her rage.

"And what if I decide not to face it? Yes, you take on everything as you always have, but you choose to, it doesn't mean I should ..."

"I know I do. Zee," Amy began softly. "I never told you ... when the hospital staff was striking a few months ago?"

"I remember," Zara replied, still shaking.

"What I never told you was that I lost a child during that strike, Zee. I lost a patient because no one had been there to check her in. Some of the striking staff prevented others from working ... from attending to what should have been an avoidable death ... it could have been treated, should have ..." Amy said, her voice faltering.

"Amy, my God, I didn't know ..."

"I didn't tell you. But I was the doctor on duty. It was my responsibility ... so you see, for months now I have been walking with this ... this question of what it is I am supposed to be doing. Well, I know that I cannot go back to the same ward with the same staff ...

some of them ... my colleagues ... friends ... who once knew suffering, Zee, they knew ... and yet when it came down to it ... for a hand to be shown, chose no better. How naïve would it be for me to say that there are no heroes or villains any more, Zee? Just those who have power and those that don't. And yes, maybe you are right after all, maybe, possibly, one must ultimately save oneself."

37

It was November and Zara reached the station just in time to catch the train. She and Michael would watch the United States election results being announced: history in the making according to every news channel.

Posters pasted to boards and tied around poles, flapped as the wind came rushing down the line. Zara counted the number of flags she could see without twisting her head: twenty-five, no, twenty-six, including the one on the lapel of the elderly woman wearing the beige hat and gloves.

As the train began the thirty-minute journey towards the city, the woman that Zara had seen on the station sat down across from her.

"Good evening," the stranger said, throwing her greeting to whoever cared to reply. Zara responded.

The mood, despite the vitriolic tenor that the election campaign had ended with, was festive, unusually so. Zara could hear voices in polite conversation, strangers even.

"The train is full this evening," the woman continued, to no one in particular.

"Fuller than usual," Zara concurred, out of some sense of responsibility against the silence.

"I wouldn't want to speak for anyone else, but this is an announcement I plan to see," she said, as the flag on her lapel rose and fell patriotically.

"You're going on your own?" Zara asked.

"I may look old, but I don't need any looking after," she said, to chortles around her as she held her handbag steady on her lap, all the while a smile played around her mouth.

"No, of course, not." Zara offered a smile in turn.

"There isn't much to get dressed up for after a certain point and don't let anyone fool you that there is," she said, fiddling with her gloves, the silver buttons with their high shine. "Yes, grandchildren are precious," she continued, "but I already have four of them. And, anyway, to be honest, they tire me. This is a little something different." She smiled fully as the man beside her joined in the conversation. Yes, grandchildren *were* blessings he agreed, but then sometimes one had to remind oneself of that, they chuckled.

At the next station a group of students climbed on board, Zara recognised some of them from campus as they spoke loudly in the corner and passed around whatever had gripped their attention on their phones.

Just before they entered the tunnel, Zara saw the same man that she had met months earlier on that very train journey, when she had offered to pay for a stranger's ticket, enter the carriage. He stalked up the aisle, and Zara noticed his agitation.

"There are no seats this evening. Why are there no seats?" he exclaimed, from the middle of the carriage.

"The election. Everyone's going to the City to watch the results coming in," the elderly woman answered.

"There should be seats," he said loudly, restlessly. Zara looked at him carefully. It was the same man alright, and yet there was something unrecognisable about him.

"We all want some of that excitement. My sister called me an hour ago, and said I should hop on the next train. What an exciting night ..." the woman continued affably.

"Exciting? Exciting?" he returned in an incredulous, sharp tone, so that taken aback, the woman went quiet and the air around them turned.

"Let me tell you ... I have seen my share of presidents," he continued, as he pulsed back and forth, back and forth on the balls of his feet like a wartime politician. "Johnson sent me to Vietnam. Nixon was a crook, Reagan was a lousy actor, and Clinton, oh boy did that guy have some problems. The Bushes ... well, best we drop the conversation right there," he said, cutting back his own line of enquiry with one hand, as he remained on his invisible podium. "No, new president, new problems. And at the end of this journey I will still have to stand in line for a place tonight. Watch young men being drafted, coming back broken, broke ..."

The atmosphere in the carriage had gone cold: everyone looked elsewhere, the students began to gaze outside, checked their phones, the old woman searched frantically in her handbag for some tissues, or a bit of candy, or a lipstick. It was the longest tunnel in the world.

"There is a war to ruin every generation ... war ruins every generation ..." he said, looking around him. "Where is that woman?" he asked checking the door and looking at Zara for the first time.

"I think perhaps she is concentrating on other things tonight," Zara replied quietly.

"Yes ... yes," he said. "I'm going now," he offered, and then he was off, checking behind him and waiting impatiently for the doors to open, as everyone exhaled and the train docked at Pennsylvania Station.

When Zara exited the subway and reached the street, she had to move slowly for all the people who had come outside. She let her feet navigate the crowds: many were speaking excitedly, others watching the large televisions in silence in the middle of an ad hoc carnival.

New York was lost in euphoria; a kind of heady madness that even that sleepless city, with its legendary lunatics foretelling the coming, had not before seen. People were out of their apartments everywhere, doors left open, televisions running full volume from all over the city so that over and again the stories repeated themselves in deafening confirmation. A new president had been elected. The fact that he was to be the first African-American president did not weigh lightly, repeated as it was over and over again. A television anchor had gone so far as to declare it a new epoch, one of tolerance and a time for transcending.

As Zara walked down the long avenue towards Michael's place, she imagined she knew this sensation. What was it? Hope? That moment when history is undone ever so slightly, and an end of an era is in sight? Or perhaps a memory of her own: the impossible high on the evening when she and her parents realised that they were free people. Impossible, because inevitably it must lead to a fall, she wanted to say out loud to the people who were standing speechless in the middle of the street, hugging strangers, to the young man on the corner whose tears were running freely as he stood by himself. It must fall.

Still, Zara walked without realising that a smile had crept onto her face.

When Zara finally reached Michael's apartment, he had barely cracked opened the door before they were nose to nose, breathing into each other, Zara's bag hanging off her shoulder and her coat still tied up to her chin and there they remained caught between arrival and lust.

Eventually Michael unhooked himself from Zara slowly, held her by her arms and asked: "So, how are you?" His tone almost casual as he pulled her into the room. "Can you believe it?" he asked.

"That was quite a welcome ..."

"I mean the election results ..."

"He won!"

"He did!"

Zara walked to the middle of the cramped room and hung her bag and coat on an old disused treadmill (where all clothes apparently were destined).

"I caught the results as they started coming in ... but I was somewhere in the subway when the final numbers came in ..." replied Zara, bashful that she had wanted to stay wrapped up in Michael's hair and smell and touch for longer.

"Well, I'm glad you're here now," he said, and stopped to look at her fully.

He meant it. For Michael there was no keeping silent when he wanted to speak. He was open as the sky. Zara watched him rub his head, turn away so that he could adjust his shorts, embarrassedly, before walking to the small counter that demarcated the kitchen area to pour her wine.

"New beginnings?"

"Yes."

"This is a new beginning, right?"

"Of course, a new president, if he does what he says he will about Guantanamo, the wars ..."

"I *also* mean: you, me," Michael said, and for effect brought his chipped mug of wine close to Zara's own.

It was the following morning, as the light made its way unapologetically into the bedroom, yellowing the darkness that had slipped around them and made falling into each other seem so easy, so right, that Zara's phone rang. She knew before she pressed the answer button what is was about. She knew because she simply did.

"Amy ..."

Aunty Rose had died, and even across an ocean Zara knew that.

38

It was implausibly lovely. A fat, cartoonish moon shone yellow over Cape Town, visible through papery clouds. Far below, the house was all quiet, with only the rush of wind through the trees, or the clinking of the tin roof to keep Zara company.

If anything, the evening seemed to have exaggerated its presence.

Zara made these observations from where she lay on the ground, her legs crooked, her toes twisted into the thick blades of grass, as she decided that she would claim the night sky as her reward for the long days that had just passed.

The flight from New York to Johannesburg had felt endless; the allotment of space for the twenty-four hour journey unfathomably mean. She had sat surrounded by a family of five, their destination a South African safari; and they'd been eager for their promised Big Five: "Elephant, leopard, rhino ... and ... what else ... lion ... and ... and ..." the small blonde head had bobbed up and down, up and down in the seat in front of her.

"Buffalo," Zara had interjected, before the child was yanked back down and away.

The attendants had passed up and down the aisle, the familiarity of their accents strangely comforting.

When exactly had she decided to return home? All Zara knew certainly was that she had arisen one morning and the decision had been there, fully formed, as if she had not mused over it; as if it had been a simple question of return or stay, consequences and repercussions left aside. She had awoken and simply known.

On the evening of the announcement of the American election results, Zara had told Michael. He had looked at her, his eyes searching her face for another, hidden explanation not found in her words.

"Why?"

"I wish I knew how to answer that question. Half of me does ... but the rest ... in part it has to do with Amy. The fact that I have some sort of responsibility to her, that we all do, to the people we love ... she's my one constant factor ..."

"I can understand that, but if you stayed, she could visit, text, email, no?"

"Michael, she will need me there soon. The police believe they may have found the woman that assaulted my aunt ... if they have, then there will be a trial and Amy will need me at her side. But, there is that other inexplicable reason."

"Loyalty? Duty?"

"Those words seem so trite now, but yes, perhaps ..."

"To your country?"

"That could be ..."

"Because it's home?"

"Yes, probably, that too."

"To sort out the thing with your dad?"

"I'm not sure ..."

Michael had nodded his understanding. Still, the sense that he had been let down sat in the silence. After all, Zara realised that Michael might well have become her reason to stay.

Zara had flown home for a weekend of sleepless nights and unbearable jetlag to be at Aunty Rose's funeral. She had promised Amy then that she would be back soon.

On her return to the USA, she had gone to see the dean, her request that Zara apply for a permanent position at the University of Berwick, gently but firmly rebuffed.

"I think you're turning down a great opportunity. It may never come again," the dean had told her, her annoyance apparent.

"It *is* a great opportunity for someone," Zara had agreed.

With her tenure at an end and an article on the Timbuktu Manuscripts about to be published in a solid journal, she considered her time in New Jersey done.

*

After the flight from New York to Johannesburg, Zara had sat in an airport holding area waiting for her connecting flight to Cape Town. She had called Amy who, despite everything, had sounded upbeat.

"What time are you arriving? You have a car, right? I'll roast a chicken, make some salads. Open this great bottle of sparkling wine I've been keeping ... we can take it down to the beach."

"Sounds wonderful Amy, but I'll get to you too late. I have some things that I must do."

They had spoken about paying a visit to the detective in charge of Aunty Rose's case. The passing months had been difficult for Amy, and her mother's death devastating. But she had begun to write letter after letter to councillors and senior police, demanding to know what progress had been made and what evidence they had against the suspect.

Amy was still very fragile, Zara knew, but if anyone could ensure justice for what had happened to Aunty Rose, it was Amy.

Amy had offered to help Zara pack and store the bulk of her father's books and albums until Zara had the heart to do something else with them. Perhaps, thereafter, they would decide what to do with the family home. They had discussed selling it, using some of the proceeds to fund a bursary scheme for scholars, The Black Family Trust, but no, that sounded too lofty for a family who was at such odds with their past. They would think of it yet; they had the time to do it since Amy was not working. This too, the cousins had spoken about.

"Maybe you could think about specialising in paediatrics. You've always wanted to, and now is the right time," Zara had said to Amy, who had remained silent. "We can talk, right? Keep the wine chilled, I'll be there late."

Being home would hold its challenges for Zara, finding work and a new place to stay. But she had already arranged to meet with Judge Ndlovu; there were many things Zara wished to know: had the judge and her father ever acknowledged their betrayals to the other, or had it simply remained a dark chapter between them? She had already called and demanded to see the documents which had been released implicating her father, and had asked what evidence the government had to indicate that her father had betrayed more than that once. Then there was Marybeth's son, Seth, who had emailed her recently and asked if they could stay in touch.

He was thinking about making a documentary about his mother and everything that had happened. Would she be in South Africa if he came down in a couple of months? She would, she'd replied.

There was much that Zara needed to understand, so that from the pieces she could create a whole story that might make some sense that would explain her father in the necessary detail. Aside from this, there was the book that Zara would finish.

And then, before long, it would be Easter and Michael would come to visit.

*

When Zara had landed in Cape Town, she'd hired a car and driven directly to her mother's grave alongside the ocean. She'd wandered for thirty minutes searching for the spot where Lena had been buried, overwhelmed with guilt that she had avoided the place for all those years. It was usually to the house that Zara went when she wanted to feel close to Lena, but today she had needed to be where Lena's bones had been laid.

The small slab above the grave read:

Lena Black: mother, wife, sister, teacher, revolutionary.

Had Bart chosen those words? Zara could not recall. She had brushed down the grass that had grown thick and long, and found a small rock on which to sit. She had wanted to truthfully, and for the first time, see her mother the way she had really been: brave, flawed and, certainly, loyal in love.

Before she had got back into the car, Zara had made a note to return to clean up the grave and to bring flowers. Perhaps she would bring a bunch from the family house. It was nearly the end of summer and the row of gladioli that she had seen being planted two summers ago would be blooming now.

*

Zara dusted the grass from her jeans.

She walked to the room where her father's things were still kept. The place was just as she had left it more than a year ago, the books that she had knocked to the floor still lying on their sides. Bart, somehow ever present through his musty collection of books, and whiffs of shoe polish.

Methodically, book for book, Zara picked each one off the floor, ran her hand along their spines, read the titles out loud, by way of an apology for having thrown them down in the first place. A book of Shakespearean sonnets, *Laughing to Keep from Crying* by Langston Hughes, dozens more, which she returned to their shelves.

A rectangle of cardboard tucked between the pages of a novel, *The Stone-Country* by Alex La Guma, slipped to the floor as she picked up the book. It was a postcard, browning at the edges, and the image of a television tower rising high above a city, beneath a full moon, seemed dated. She checked the postmark: January 4, 1990, but there was no name, nor a return address. All the postcard had on it were the following words:

During our years together, perhaps we both made one terrible, egregious mistake. Let us each forgive.

Zara sat with the postcard for a long time, running her finger over the words, saying them out loud to herself. Of course, she knew that they had been written by Marybeth, and she realised more than anything, that these were the words she had most needed to hear: that Bart had made one mistake.

She knew too that it had been Marybeth's forgiveness that she had wanted for her father. Still, she didn't think that she was ready to excuse what Bart had done, but perhaps it was time to see her father in a different light. After all, in her father's defence, he had helped to raise Zara to be non-racist, non-violent, bigoted only against bigots. Bart had sacrificed his career for what he had done. He had shown remorse. And surely, surely, that must count for something?

Zara finished straightening Bart's books, his records and CDs. She had never before noticed the turntable beneath a pile of old records, covered in layers of plastic. Had she packed it there? It appeared to be in good condition and Zara plugged it in, stunned when the system lit up. Picking a record from the shelves, one Bart might have approved of, Zara cleaned it carefully with the back of her sweater. She placed the album on the player, brought down the needle and walked back into the garden, the postcard held delicately between her fingers.

The watchman who had allowed her in, would not make his rounds for another hour, so Zara would continue to lie supine beneath the night sky, in the garden that her grandmother, and her mother, had once tended with such love.

ACKNOWLEDGMENTS

I am especially grateful to Micah Naidoo for his love, countless readings of this novel, friendship and support; and of course, to Milan.

Thank you to my readers Janine Fraser, Nadia Davids, Rejáne Woodroffe, as well as Isabel Hofmeyr, Kelwyn Sole and Patrick Flanery for their generosity and guidance. My thanks to Colleen Higgs of Modjaji Books for acts of faith offered to me and countless others, and, to Karen Jennings for editing.

Much gratitude to everyone who provided information, friendship and many other kindnesses along the way: Greg Davids for his impeccable knowledge of Jazz, Robert and Marjorie Davids, Shereen Murphy, Dot Murphy for her example of what a teacher should be, Fiona Davids, Janine and Barry Fraser, Keri, Miles, Callum and Harleigh. My thanks, always, to Zenda Woodman and Ashraf Johaardien.

Thank you to the Arts and Culture Trust for a Development Grant that assisted in the production of this book.

Thank you to A P Watt at United Agents LLP on behalf of Nadine Gordimer, for their kind permission to quote from *Burger's Daughter* by Nadine Gordimer on page 172 of this novel.

The authors and books that enabled an understanding of South African society after the discovery of diamonds, and of Cape Town during the twentieth century are: William H. Worger for *South Africa's City of Diamonds: Mine Workers and Monopoly Capitalism in Kimberley, 1867 – 1895*, Yale Historical Publications, June 1987; Harold Jack Simons and Ray Esther Simons for *Class and Colour in South Africa 1850 – 1950*, Volume 25 of Penguin African Library, Penguin 1969; Antony Thomas for *Rhodes: The Race for Africa* by, St Martin's Press, 1997; Vivian Bickford-Smith for *Ethnic Pride and Racial Prejudice in Victorian Cape Town*, Cambridge University Press, 2003.